HE WAS HERS. . . . BUT FOR HOW LONG?

His kiss was rough and demanding, his hands roaming freely over her body, causing her to lose that last semblance of control that still remained. She pressed closer to him, closer still, wanting their bodies to join, to be one.

"Lee, my lovely Lee," he murmured.

"Oh, Paul," she gasped, "don't stop—please don't stop."

"My sweet darling," he whispered, his mouth brushing over her ear, "is this what you want? Is it?"

"Yes, yes," she gasped. "Oh, yes!"

CANDLELIGHT ECSTASY ROMANCES™

STAGES OF LOVE

Beverly Sommers

A CANDLELIGHT ECSTASY ROMANCE™

Published by
Dell Publishing Co., Inc.
1 Dag Hammarskjold Plaza
New York, New York 10017

Dell ® TM 681510, Dell Publishing Co., Inc.

Candlelight Ecstasy Romance™ is a trademark of
Dell Publishing Co., Inc., New York, New York.

ISBN: 0–440–18363–4

Printed in the United States of America
First printing—November 1981

Dear Reader:

In response to your enthusiasm for Candlelight Ecstasy Romances™, we are now increasing the number of titles per month from two to three.

We are pleased to offer you sensuous novels set in America, depicting modern American women and men as they confront the provocative problems of a modern relationship.

Throughout the history of the Candlelight line, Dell has tried to maintain a high standard of excellence, to give you the finest in reading pleasure. It is now and will remain our most ardent ambition.

Vivian Stephens
Editor
Candlelight Romances

STAGES OF LOVE

CHAPTER ONE

Lee could scarcely contain her excitement as the plane circled Kennedy Airport, preparing to land. As she strained across her seat partner, trying to see out the window, tall buildings intermittently came into view, then vanished, and soon they were taxiing down the runway before coming to a stop. Although the FASTEN SEATBELTS sign was still on, people were already jamming the aisles in an effort to be the first off. Lee waited until the crowd thinned a bit before gathering up her purse and suit jacket and retrieving her small overnighter from under her seat. She had packed very lightly, just the one case she had been allowed to carry on the plane, which meant she wouldn't have to wait in line for the luggage to be unloaded.

The telegram had advised her to take a taxi directly to the theater, stating she would be reimbursed for the cost. As she left the terminal building, the heat hit her with a force that left her feeling instantly wilted. She spotted the line of taxis and headed for the first, thankful to the driver for having his motor running and his cab air-conditioned.

"Where to, lady?" queried the driver.

"Just a moment," said Lee, getting the letter out of her purse to check the address. "The Village Playhouse on West Twelfth Street. Do you know where that is?"

"No problem." The driver took off like a contender in the Indianapolis 500, causing Lee to consider leaping over the seat, wresting the wheel from his hands, and demonstrating to him how a sensible, sane driver handled a vehicle. Instead she leaned back in the seat, her eyes on the letter rather than on the road ahead, thinking the man wouldn't last two minutes on a California freeway.

Lee had read the letter so many times she practically had it memorized; nonetheless, she glanced through it one more time. It stated that the Village Playhouse was looking forward to doing the first production of *Alekos*. They would provide room, board, airfare, and a stipend of two hundred dollars to enable her to be present during the rehearsal period. A contract had been enclosed, which she had immediately signed and returned. It seemed to be a standard form letter, but at the bottom a personal note had been scrawled.

"I look forward to directing your *Alekos*. This is the most exciting play to come my way in a long time."

It was signed "Paul Devon."

She looked out the window at the unfamiliar landscape. Nary a palm tree in sight, nor a pastel-colored house for that matter. Just endless apartment complexes and a view of the Manhattan skyline in the distance.

Lee had been in a constant state of excitement since receiving the letter; it was the most momentous thing that had happened to her in her twenty-eight years. When it had arrived, she had immediately telephoned her department head, who was almost as thrilled as she.

"That's marvelous, Lee," he had enthused. "And what a coup for the department—you're going to put Orange Coast College on the map. Drama students will be flocking here when they learn about our having a Broadway playwright on the faculty."

"Off-Broadway," interjected Lee.

"Maybe for now, but next it will be Broadway."

Lee laughed. "I doubt whether many people are going to hear about it."

"Are you kidding? I'm going to start advertising the fact immediately."

"I'll probably miss the first few weeks of school," Lee told him, hoping it wouldn't be a breach of her contract.

"Not to worry—I'll take over your classes personally until your return. And in exchange . . ."

"Just name it!"

"I expect you to have a hit."

"I'll try my hardest," Lee promised.

And she would, too, she thought to herself now. It was her big chance to get out of teaching and be able to write full time. Not that she didn't enjoy her job, but it was not satisfying to her in the way that writing was. And while she had written short stories and even some poetry, it was playwriting that really fired her enthusiasm. To hear the words she wrote spoken by actors, to see her play come alive on the stage, seemed to her to be the most exciting thing she could imagine. And now it was going to be done, and not just by a local, nonprofessional group, but one of the better known off-Broadway theaters.

There were some good playhouses in California, but to Lee New York was synonymous with theater, and so, six months before, she had sent a copy of her play to the Village Playhouse after reading an article about the prestigious off-Broadway theater that had given so many well-known playwrights their starts. She had almost forgotten about it by the time the letter arrived. Not totally—it was always there in the back of her mind—but almost.

The light in the cab suddenly dimmed and Lee looked up to see that they were driving through a tunnel. When the taxi emerged, she realized they were in Manhattan, which to her was the "real" New York City.

Minutes after that they were pulling up in front of the theater, and Lee paid the driver what seemed to her to be an exorbitant amount, and got out. It was a small theater in a lovely old brick building on a quiet street. She glanced up at the marquee, half expecting to see her name there, but it still advertised the play that was currently running.

11

A few more weeks, though, she thought, and it will say ALEKOS up there in big letters.

She gave her name to the young man in the box office and he looked her over in surprise. Lee surmised by his expression that they had expected someone older and hoped that this didn't mean she wouldn't be taken seriously.

"*You're* Lee Masterson?"

She nodded, wondering if he was going to ask for some identification.

He went around to the door of the theater and opened it, waving her inside. "I'm Frank Rakas," he told her, shaking her hand. "They call me the business manager to make up for my small salary. Actually I just sell tickets and answer the phone." He noticed her suitcase and took it from her. "The members of the board are in the conference room waiting for you. I'm going to take you in personally—I can't wait to see the expressions on their faces."

Lee followed him upstairs, wondering what the big deal was about her age. There were plenty of playwrights as young as she being produced.

Five male heads turned as one to look at her when Frank led her into the conference room. To a man they appraised her slowly from her shoulder-length blond hair, down past her slim body clad in a white linen suit and black silk blouse, down further past the length of firm, tanned legs and ending up at high-heeled sandals. Lee felt decidedly uncomfortable and briefly wondered if her clothes were wrong. She thought New Yorkers would dress with more sophistication, but the men were all casually attired in jeans and sport shirts.

Frank grinned at the reaction of the board. "Gentlemen," he announced in a voice clearly trained for the stage, "I have the pleasure of presenting to you, Lee Masterson—our new . . . lady playwright . . . straight from the Coast."

The shock in the room was palpable. Four of the men

tried unsuccessfully to hide their surprise. The fifth, whom Lee had noticed immediately, not so much for the Mickey Mouse T-shirt he was sporting as for his virile good looks, narrowed cool gray eyes for a moment, then visibly relaxed and started to chuckle. "Good try, Frank—now tell us who she really is. One of your girl friends who wants to audition?" He turned skeptical eyes on Lee. "Better yet, can you type? We could use a decent typist around here."

Lee was totally confused at the reaction she had caused, but not so confused that she didn't understand an insult when she heard one. "Of course I type. Don't all women? I find as a writer typing is an absolute necessity." She saw her adversary flush and gave a smile of satisfaction. "Gentlemen," she addressed the four other board members, "I don't know what you were expecting, but I *am* Lee Masterson."

A bearish man of about forty with a head of frizzy salt-and-pepper hair stood up and held out his hand to her. "It's a pleasure meeting you, Ms. Masterson. I'm John Melfi, production director of the Playhouse. I must confess we had expected a man. Not that it makes any difference at all"—he turned to the other board members who, all save one, nodded in agreement—"but you understand our surprise."

Lee was as confused as the men looked. "Why would you assume I was a man? Lee is certainly very common as a woman's name. Actually it's Merrilee—Merrilee Masterson—but I've always been called Lee."

Her adversary, whose eyes had never left her, spoke up. "It wasn't the name. I think if you had submitted a typical woman's script, we would have assumed you were female. But I find it hard to believe *Alekos* was written by a woman. It's a man's play; it has a man's theme, a man's viewpoint, the male characters are much more deeply drawn than the female . . . in short, Merrilee, or whoever you are, I think this is a hoax."

Frank and the board members were looking at Lee in

consternation. She gave the obnoxious man what she hoped was her haughtiest stare. "Might I know your name?"

"Paul Devon—as though you didn't know." He answered her with biting sarcasm.

Lee reached into her purse and withdrew the letter, tossing it on the table in front of Mr. Devon. She then removed her wallet, opened it and extracted her driver's license, library card, and several credit cards, tossing them slowly, one by one, on top of the letter.

Paul Devon picked up the driver's license, glanced at the name, then checked her appearance against the photo. His anger seemed to collapse. "There's no way I'm working with a female playwright," he said wearily to the other members.

John Melfi turned to Frank. "Why don't you take Ms. Masterson down to your office—fix her a cup of coffee."

Lee stood firm, not intending to give up her chance to be produced so easily. "I'd like to know right now how things stand, Mr. Melfi. I accepted your terms, signed your contract, and flew all the way here from California. Are you *all* unwilling to work with a woman, or only your temperamental director? Perhaps you have a woman director who would not feel it beneath her dignity to work with me."

John Melfi took charge. "Frank, how about coffee for all of us." Frank, a disappointed look on his face, reluctantly left the room. Mr. Melfi looked at Lee. "Ms. Masterson—that's a mouthful. Do you mind if I call you Lee?"

"Not at all," Lee assured him.

"Let me introduce you to the others." He turned first to Dennis Embry and Norman Rhodes, the resident playwrights, two young men not much older than herself whose works she had taught in her course. "And this," he said, putting his hand on the shoulder of an older man in his fifties, "is Milo Jordan, our artistic director." He held

14

out a chair for her. "Sit down, Lee. Now that the shock's worn off, I think we should get down to business."

Paul Devon shifted in his chair. "The shock has *not* worn off."

John sighed. "Don't pull a prima donna act on us, Paul."

"I'd be glad to take over the direction of this play," Milo Jordan offered. "I have no objections to working with a woman. And to be realistic, I think this is going to turn out to be a good thing. The critics have given us a lot of flak over the years for never having produced a woman writer. Now's our chance to prove we're not male chauvinists."

Lee almost laughed aloud at that. If *they* weren't male chauvinists, then there was no such animal.

"And we accomplish it," Milo went on, "with a play we all were enthusiastic about."

"Right. Not at all the usual thing we get women submitting to us," put in Norman Rhodes.

Lee started to fume. "So I'm to be your token woman, is that it?"

"Would you mind very much?" John asked her anxiously.

"Whether I mind or not," Lee answered, "there's not much I can do about it. Your prejudice against women playwrights seems too deeply ingrained to change overnight."

"You're forgetting one thing." They all turned to look at Paul. "Not only am I supposed to be directing her play—"

"I'd be glad to direct it," Milo broke in.

Paul gave him an angry look. "This is *my* kind of play, Milo. You do the comedies, *I* do the political dramas."

"It's not meant to be a political play," Lee informed him.

"Before I was interrupted," Paul went on, "I was about to remind you that not only am I supposed to be directing the play, but I'm also providing room and board to the playwright."

Lee felt a sinking sensation in her stomach. She was sure that anyone who had taken such an instant dislike to her as Paul Devon had, would certainly not want her around all the time as his houseguest. She wondered briefly whether she could get a flight back to California that night.

"You've got a duplex, Paul," John reminded him. "Lee won't be in your way. With the rehearsal schedule, you two will rarely be at home except to catch a few hours' sleep anyway." He turned to Lee. "Do you object to the arrangement?"

Lee thought about it for a moment. Her first impulse had been to tear up the contract and throw it in their faces. Or at least in one of their faces. Two things stopped her. She didn't have the contract, and, more than anything in the world, she wanted to see her play produced. Whether she stayed in Paul Devon's duplex or the local YWCA was immaterial to her; it was strictly a business arrangement. She could see that Paul was not about to back down from his hostile stance. It was up to her, the novice, to make an attempt at conciliation. She looked at Paul and smiled, a smile that would have been guaranteed to melt even his heart, if a glint of anger hadn't remained in her green eyes. "Mr. Devon," she said to him in a deceptively sweet voice, "I was truly honored when I heard you were to direct my play. To have my first work directed by someone as notable as yourself surpassed my wildest dreams. If you would be willing to reconsider, I can promise you I will be your willing apprentice. As for my staying with you, I'd gladly sleep in a corner on the floor for the privilege of working with you."

A look of disbelief had slowly come over Paul's face as he listened to her speech. She realized he hadn't been taken in by it at all, but she also noticed the others had, and when Paul looked around the table for support and instead saw the benevolent smiles being bestowed on Lee, he shook his head and leaned back in his chair, eyeing her warily once again. Then a glint came into his own eyes. "Sleep on the floor, Ms. Masterson? Don't be absurd. You'll have the bedroom next to mine. We'll be working very closely, after all."

John looked at him with disapproval. "I think you owe Lee an apology, Paul."

Paul raised an eyebrow in surprise. "Oh, come on, John. Since when have you known me to go for fluffy-headed blondes?"

"This fluffy-headed blonde wrote the play you told me was brilliant," John reminded him.

Lee caught her breath at the word "brilliant" and chose to ignore the "fluffy-headed blonde" part.

Paul laughed, and the tension around the table immediately eased. "Don't let it go to your head. I'm noted for getting carried away with plays that the critics end up demolishing."

"Not all of them," said Dennis Embry, who had had some of his own plays successfully directed by Paul.

Paul stood up. "Since Frank seems to have forgotten about our coffee, and since this whole thing has managed to give me a headache, I suggest we take care of any business later. I'll take Ms. Masterson home and let her get settled in. Auditions are first thing in the morning, right, John?"

John nodded.

Lee stood up, said her good-byes to the other men, then followed Paul out of the room. He stood in the hallway for a moment, looking down at her.

"In addition to being a passable writer, you're also a pretty good actress," he said, trying to goad her, but Lee, knowing she was going to have to spend the evening in his company, decided to curb her tendency to say exactly what she thought.

17

Getting no reaction out of her, he started down the stairs. "Where's your luggage?"

"I think Frank put it in his office."

He turned into Frank's cubbyhole and was right back out with her one piece of luggage. "This it?"

She nodded.

"One small suitcase to last you a few weeks?"

"I didn't think I'd be going out anywhere. Anyway, I've heard New York has clothing stores."

He chuckled. "You heard right."

"Mr. Devon?"

"Call me Paul—I don't think I can manage that 'Ms. Masterson' much longer."

"Would it be all right for me to see the theater?"

He set down her suitcase. "We meant to take you on a tour of the place, but it kind of got lost in the shuffle. Follow me."

It looked perfect to Lee. Not too large, a good view of the stage from every seat in the house, and the set for the current production was lovely, an exact replica of a large country kitchen complete with fireplace. Something seemed to be missing, though, and she finally realized what it was."

"Where's the curtain?" she asked Paul.

"Curtain? Nobody uses a curtain anymore."

Lee thought about the college productions where she always experienced a thrill when the curtain opened. "But in my play, where I wrote Curtain at the end of the acts, what happens if there's no curtain?"

"The lights go out."

"Don't any of the theaters have curtains anymore?"

"A few." He grinned at her. "When we take your play to Broadway, we'll request a theater with a curtain, okay?"

She wasn't sure whether he was kidding or whether he thought *Alekos* had a chance of making it to Broadway, but just the thought of it was enough to put Lee in a trance as she pictured the opening night of her play on Broadway.

"Come on!" Paul broke into her reverie. "Don't worry, you'll see enough of this place to last you a lifetime."

Lee turned and followed him out of the theater.

CHAPTER TWO

Paul led her down the street at a rapid pace, not giving her a chance even to look around.

"Are we taking a subway?" she asked him.

"I only live a few blocks from here."

She was disappointed. "I was hoping to ride on a subway."

"What are you, crazy? No one *hopes* to ride on a subway. What you hope is that you can avoid getting anywhere near one!" He slowed his pace. "Am I going too fast for you?"

"I guess I'm used to driving."

"Yeah, you Californians are all in bad shape." He reconsidered. "Not that you *look* out of shape."

"I knew what you meant."

He speeded up again, not noticing she was forced to jog to keep up with him. "After this I'll wear my running shoes," she gasped as he slowed down for a red light.

He looked down at her. "Listen, you're supposed to be getting room and board at my place, but I don't cook. Do you?"

"No."

"Good—we'll eat out."

He took off again and it occurred to her that he walked very much like the cab driver had driven, as though he were in a race.

"You like Italian?"

She couldn't figure out what he meant. "I find the language lyrical. And I like Italian movies."

"You being sarcastic?"

"No!"

"I meant food. Do you like Italian food?"

"I like spaghetti."

"I guess that's something." He suddenly made a quick turn and was seated at a table in a sidewalk café. "Sit down—we were lucky to find a table."

She looked around. "Are there tables inside?"

"Sure, but we were lucky to get one out here."

She felt perspiration running down her neck. It was still just as hot as when she had stepped off the plane. "Is it air-conditioned inside?"

"You don't want to eat in an air-conditioned place," he informed her. "You'd just feel hotter when you came back out."

Lee didn't know how she could possibly feel any hotter. A horrible thought occurred to her. "Is your apartment air-conditioned?"

He looked at her as though she were crazy and she was very afraid the answer was going to be in the negative.

"Of course! You think I could sleep in heat like this?"

Lee gave in and sat down, looking forward to getting the meal over with so that they could get to his air-conditioned apartment and she could change into something cooler.

The waiter came by and Paul waved aside the menus. "I'll order for us, okay with you?"

"I can order for myself." If there was anything Lee found annoying, it was domineering men.

"Maybe in McDonald's you can order for yourself, but if you think Italian food is spaghetti, you're incapable of doing it here."

Paul ordered quickly, the food sounding unrecognizable to Lee. There was again a glint in her eyes when she said to him sweetly, "As long as we're disagreeing anyway, I

22

wish you'd explain that remark you made about my play having a male theme."

He looked at her with genuine interest for the first time. "Maybe you'd tell me what you think the theme is?"

"I *know* what the theme is; I wrote the play. The theme happens to be freedom, and I don't think that's a subject that is confined to men."

He laughed. "I know a lot of men who'd give you an argument about that. Particularly married men!"

"If you could refrain from being flippant, I'd also like to point out to you that *Alekos* is *not* a political play."

"Are you telling me you wrote that play with no conscious notion of what you were writing about?"

"You know, Paul, I really find you insulting. I knew *exactly* what I was writing about. I was writing about heroism and freedom, and just because I placed it in the context of a political movement in no way relegates it to a propagandist play."

"Hey, wait a minute." He was interrupted by the waiter setting down a bottle of wine and two glasses. He looked at Lee. "Red wine okay?"

"Sure."

He poured them each a glass and she drank some down quickly, immediately feeling its relaxing effect.

"As I was saying, political and propagandist are not synonymous, young lady. I find the whole Greek resistance movement very viable dramatically, and what happened in Greece with the Colonels is happening in other places today. Don't get the idea I thought you were spouting propaganda—if I had, I wouldn't have called your play brilliant. Propaganda plays are never brilliant, they're usually never more than mediocre. But a strong drama in a political context, that's something else. And before your head gets completely turned by my use of 'brilliant,' let me warn you there are many areas where revisions are going to be needed. It's a very good first draft, but it needs work."

(23

"It's my *third* draft."

"Whatever."

She smiled at him. "You don't know how great it is to have someone to discuss my play with—someone who's interested. I liked it when I wrote it, but I had no idea whether anyone else would. That's the only bad thing about writing—you do it in a vacuum."

"Haven't you had a reading of your play?"

Lee shook her head. "I thought of having my students do a reading of it, but decided that would be taking advantage of my position."

"That's what's great about our group at the Playhouse. The resident playwrights get a chance to have readings by experienced actors all during the writing process. After the readings we critique it, then the writer goes back to work."

Lee thought it was too bad the group seemed so opposed to having a woman member. She couldn't think of anything she'd like more than to be a part of such a group. She knew there were probably many such groups in the city, though, and maybe she would be able to find one that didn't restrict itself to men.

Salads were placed in front of them and a large basket of bread was set on the table. Lee had hardly begun to eat when the main course arrived along with bowls of spaghetti. She buttered a piece of bread, quickly finished off her salad, then started in on the spaghetti.

Paul was watching her, an amused expression on his face. "Didn't they feed you on the plane?"

She nodded, quickly swallowing the food in her mouth. "Sure. Twice." She was about to take another mouthful of spaghetti when his hand reached across the table and clutched her wrist.

"You haven't tried the veal scallopini."

Lee glanced down at the strange-looking food. "Oh, is that what it's called?"

"Try it!"

24

He released her wrist and she dropped the spaghetti back on her plate and moved the fork over to push around the unfamiliar food. "I don't really care for veal," she informed him, thinking if he had let her order her own food this wouldn't have happened.

His eyes narrowed. "You'll like it cooked like this. The chef's great—I eat here all the time."

Lee defiantly went back to the spaghetti, managing to get the fork to her mouth with no interference this time.

"No veal scallopini, no dessert," he threatened her.

Lee ignored him, wondering if he realized how much it infuriated her to be treated like a child. The rest of the meal was quite to her liking; if he liked the veal scallopini so much, he was welcome to hers.

"What's the matter, you afraid to try something new? Where's your spirit of adventure?" He was leaning across the table now, regarding her like a lab specimen.

Lee decided since they had gotten off to a bad start at the theater she had better not antagonize him further. Only she didn't want the appeasement to have to take the form of eating that strange concoction in front of her.

She gave him an innocent look. "Do you know, Paul, when I was a child I thought veals were animals."

"Veal is very young calf."

"I know that now." She paused, then added carefully, "But when I was a child I thought they were cute little animals with lots of fur and I didn't want to eat them." She smiled at him, certain he would understand.

He didn't.

"Well, now you're an adult, Lee, and you know they're *not* little furry animals, and you've got about ten seconds to try the veal scallopini before I personally get out of my chair and come over there and feed you!"

"You really have a temper, don't you?" she asked him, but the look on his face finally induced her to try a bite of the disputed dish.

He sat perfectly still, waiting for her reaction as she

25

slowly chewed up the portion in her mouth, then washed it down with wine. When she took her second mouthful, he could contain himself no longer.

"Well? What do you think?"

She stared back at him for a moment, wondering if he would have actually force-fed her. She felt she could see his blood pressure rising as he waited for her verdict. Lee broke the long silence. "It's okay—really not much taste at all. I was afraid it was going to be spicy."

She pretended not to notice his stunned reaction as she quickly finished the veal scallopini. There was no way she was going to give him the satisfaction of hearing it was one of the most delicious dishes she had ever tasted. Not after he had treated her like a child. Fluffy-headed blonde, indeed!

He finally found his voice. "You're a nut, you know that?"

"But a brilliant playwright."

He lighted a cigarette. "You're never going to let me forget that, are you? Anyway, I didn't say you were a brilliant playwright, I said your play was brilliant. And I only said that because we were trying to decide between your play and a comedy, and I felt like directing the fall production. In any event," he added, "it doesn't matter. With my brilliant direction, no one will know the difference."

She saw by the gleam in his eye that he was trying to get a rise out of her, so she quickly stifled the retort she was about to make, instead smiling sweetly at him. "Do I get dessert now?"

"Don't think you can fool me with that ingenue smile of yours when your green eyes are setting off sparks," he cautioned her, and she made a mental note to wear sunglasses around him in the future. He was far too perceptive.

"I *would* like some dessert."

He got the attention of their waiter. "Something light

after that big meal?" Paul asked her. "How about some fruit?"

Lee ignored him and spoke directly to the waiter. "Do you have any chocolate cake?"

She was assured that they did indeed have chocolate cake.

"With, perhaps, some ice cream on top?"

"I better learn how to cook," Paul muttered. "Otherwise you're going to cost me a fortune in food the way you eat."

He didn't give her time to sit and relax after the meal, but jumped up as soon as she had finished the last bite of cake and moved down the street at his former brisk pace.

"I didn't expect New York to look like this," she said to him when they stopped for a light at the corner. "Tree-lined streets, quaint little buildings—where are all the skyscrapers?"

"This is Greenwich Village." He turned and pointed up. "See that building?"

Lee nodded.

"That's the Empire State Building." He turned her in the other direction. "See those two towers up there?"

She nodded.

"That's the World Trade Center. Okay, satisfied? End of tour!"

They walked the rest of the distance to his apartment in silence.

His apartment consisted of the top two floors of a brownstone situated on a quiet block of the Village quite close to the theater.

He opened the door and motioned for Lee to precede him into the apartment. Before she had gotten her two feet inside, she experienced an overwhelming sense of claustrophobia. Everywhere she looked was furniture: tables overflowing with magazines, desks overflowing with papers, couches and chairs piled high with pillows. Newspapers were stacked against every wall; not one inch of wall space was showing between what seemed to be floor-to-ceiling pictures. Every available surface had its share of clutter. It reminded Lee of a second-hand store where the owners kept taking in new merchandise but never made a sale.

He was watching her, waiting for her reaction. She tried hard to think of something to say, but words failed her.

"Well, what do you think of the living room?" he asked at last.

Living room? she thought to herself. Where on earth could a person do any living? "You certainly have a lot of . . ." She rejected several possibilities that came to mind.

"Memorabilia." He supplied the word for her.

To Lee's mind, last week's newspapers did not constitute memorabilia, but she guessed if he hung on to them long enough they might some day qualify as such.

"People never believe it when they see it." There was a note of pride in his voice.

Understandably, thought Lee. She certainly didn't believe it.

"I'm really lucky to have this kind of space in New York," Paul was saying to her. "It's more room than I need, but I'm the one who always gets stuck putting people up for the Playhouse."

More room than he needed? Lee was sure he could fill every available corner of Madison Square Garden with just the junk in the living room alone. "Sorry you got stuck with me," she commented wryly.

He gave her a chagrined look. "I'm not noted for my diplomacy."

"I could tell that as soon as we met."

"But then neither are you, it would appear." He gave the room a fond once-over before leading her out into the hallway. "I've decided to let you use my bedroom while you're here."

"I don't want you to put yourself out for me," Lee said quickly, wondering what the bedroom could possibly look like and thinking perhaps she should find a hotel room at her own expense.

"It'll work out better that way. My bedroom is upstairs, and there's a bath up there, too, so you'll have complete privacy. I can sleep in the den down here; half the time I fall asleep in there when I'm working at night anyway."

She followed him up the stairs to a spacious bedroom, the complete opposite of the living room, as it held nothing but a bed. No bedside table, not a lamp in sight, nothing containing drawers. Just one large, in fact she would describe it as gigantic, bed. Now if he would just move some of the furniture from the living room upstairs . . .

"This will be fine," she murmured.

The bed was unmade, which looked to be its normal condition. Paul made a half-hearted attempt to straighten it, then turned to her. "Do you mind changing the sheets yourself?"

Mind? She would insist upon it.

For the first time since she had met him, Paul was looking ill at ease. "Well, I guess you've had a long day. You'll probably want to turn in."

Lee glanced at her watch. "Turn in? It's only five o'clock in California. But even if it were eight, I wouldn't feel like turning in."

He looked at his own watch. "It's just that I have some work to do."

Lee decided to take pity on him. She had brought along the first draft of her new play and could use the time to start on the revisions. "That's all right, Paul. Just pretend I'm not here and do what you normally do. I can amuse myself."

He looked so relieved Lee began to feel insulted. She thought it unfortunate that he wasn't in the least attracted to her, because as far as she was concerned, she would really like to get to know him better. But then she had always had a weakness for men with shaggy dark hair and cool gray eyes and slim, athletic-looking bodies and wry senses of humor and volatile tempers. She caught herself staring at him and turned away.

"If you're sure you can amuse yourself." He sounded impatient to leave, which did nothing for her ego.

"Positive. Go do your work, I'll be fine."

"Good. I'll see you in the morning then. We should be at the theater by ten."

"Fine."

He left without another word, almost running in his eagerness to be away from her. She realized belatedly that he hadn't given her the clean sheets. She opened the door to the one closet and found a set on the shelf. They were lime green with purple butterflies, and she wondered at his taste. But they were clean, and she had no objection to sleeping on purple butterflies.

She made up the bed, finding a hamper in the bathroom for the dirty sheets, then unpacked her few things and hung them up. She took a shower, which felt marvelous, and changed into jeans and a blouse, putting aside her suit to take to the cleaners.

With nothing left to do, she got out the first draft of her play. The dim overhead light was inadequate to work under, and she wondered if he would mind her borrowing one of the lamps from the living room. Whether he minded or not, she decided to help herself to one. If she was going to be spending the next few weeks sleeping in the room, she would definitely need a reading lamp.

She went downstairs. Passing a closed door on the way to the living room, she heard a familiar sound coming from within. Without stopping to think, she opened the door and looked inside. Paul was seated on a couch in front of a giant TV screen.

Lee's eyes widened. "You said you had work to do."

He jumped in surprise. "Well . . ."

"You're watching baseball!"

He looked like a child caught with his hand in the cookie jar. "I know it looks that way. . . ."

"Because it *is* that way." She took a step inside. "*I* want to watch."

He didn't take it in at once. "*You* like baseball?"

"Why shouldn't I like baseball?"

"Well, you're a writer . . ."

"Baseball's a director's sport, is that it?" She eyed the can he was holding. "I also like beer."

"Help yourself—there's more in the refrigerator."

Lee found the kitchen, which was surprisingly neat even considering the fact that he didn't cook. The refrigerator held three different kinds of beer, a package of cheese in individually wrapped slices, and an opened bag of pretzels. She helped herself to all three and went back to the den, settling down on the rug in front of the TV. She was very glad not to have to do any work that night after all.

"I think that was pretty sneaky of you," she remarked when the first commercial came on.

"How was I supposed to know you liked baseball?"

"You could have asked."

He reached out a hand for some pretzels. "Actually, what we should be doing is discussing your play tonight."

"You're probably right. I have a lot of things I want to talk over with you."

"It's not as though it's a playoff game, or anything." She took a sip of her beer. "Yeah."

He reached for some of the cheese. "What do you think? Should we turn off the set and do some work?"

But by that time the commercial was over, so she ignored him.

CHAPTER THREE

There was already a line of actors extending around the block when they arrived at the theater the next morning. Some of them called out greetings to Paul as he hustled Lee through the stage-door entrance. Frank was there taking down the names of some actors who were already inside.

"See if you can rustle us up some coffee," Paul said to her. "I want to talk to John before we get started."

Frank winked at her. "Don't take offense, it's not 'cause you're a woman. He bosses everyone around—directors are like that."

"That's all right," Lee assured him. "I'd do anything for a cup of coffee right now. Eating breakfast doesn't seem to be one of his habits." When Paul had knocked on her door that morning to awaken her, he had allowed her only fifteen minutes to get ready before they had to leave for the theater. She had quickly showered, dressed in a cotton skirt, T-shirt, and low-heeled sandals, then had brushed her hair back in a ponytail. She knew it made her look younger, but it would also be cooler, and she wasn't trying to impress anyone today.

Frank showed her where the coffeepot was already plugged in and she poured two cups of coffee. "Where do I go now?" she asked Frank.

He pointed out the way and promised to bring her a couple of donuts the first chance he got.

Lee was walking carefully across the stage, head down

so as not to spill the coffee, when she bumped into someone before she saw him. She did, however, see a dark stain spreading on the young man's white pants. She looked up, ready to offer a sincere apology. What she saw left her speechless. Outside of a couple of statues of Greek gods, the man had the most incredibly beautiful face she had ever seen. Dark curly hair, features that could have been chiseled by Michelangelo, dark eyes framed by lashes an inch long, and, as she lowered her gaze, a body dressed in a form-fitting shirt and tight pants that was the nearest thing to perfection she had ever come across.

He seemed to sense her dilemma. "Can I help you carry that?" he offered.

Lee found her voice. "I'm so sorry—I spilled it all over your pants, they're ruined."

"Don't worry about it—it's my fault for not wearing my usual jeans. If it hadn't been you, it would have been something else."

His voice was as beautiful as his face and she waited for him to go on, wanting to hear its mesmerizing quality again.

"What part are you auditioning for?" he asked her.

"Oh . . . I'm not an actress." Lee realized instantly that he was, of course, an actor. What else with those looks, that voice.

"I was sure you were, you're so darned pretty. If I were a director I'd cast you just so I could look at you all day."

Lee had never felt less pretty in her life. Next to him she was certain she faded to just plain ordinary. But he was smiling at her, and certainly sounded sincere, so she had sense enough not to give him an argument about it and maybe shatter his illusions.

Paul shouted out, "Where's the coffee?" She looked out over the footlights and saw him seated several rows back, looking at her with impatience.

"I better go," Lee said to the gorgeous young man,

wishing she could think of something more brilliant to say so he'd remember her.

He gave her a warm smile. "I better get to work too, try to familiarize myself with the lines. I hope to see you later."

"Me too," murmured Lee to his retreating back.

"What were you doing with Jesse?" Paul muttered as she handed him his coffee.

"If you mean the young man on the stage, I was spilling coffee all over him."

Paul gave a bark of laughter. "You always that hard on actors?"

"It wasn't intentional," Lee snapped. "His name is Jesse? Jesse what?"

"Richard Jesse."

"He's beautiful," Lee breathed, picturing in her mind the young man's face.

"He's a nice-looking kid," Paul admitted. "Got talent too."

Lee glanced over at Paul. "I'd like to see him play Alekos."

"Alekos? No way! He hasn't the experience to carry the lead. Anyway, you haven't even heard him read yet."

"I heard him talk," said Lee dreamily, remembering the young man's voice.

"Can't I leave you alone two minutes without your falling in love with some actor?" Paul sounded annoyed.

Lee felt herself blushing. "I didn't fall in love," she protested. "I just think he'd be right for Alekos, that's all." And he was a lot nicer to me than you've been, she thought crossly.

"Well, you'll be hearing young Adonis read along with a few hundred others." Paul handed her a yellow legal pad and a pencil. "Make notes of the ones you like and we'll discuss them at lunch."

Lee's play was based upon a true incident. In 1968, when the Colonels were in power in Greece, a young student named Alexandros Panagoulis made an attempted assassination on the dictator, Colonel Papadopoulos. When they arrested Alekos, it was found that he was the head of Greek Resistance, the student underground. While in prison, he smuggled out his poems, written in blood, and won the Viareggio Award for Poetry, becoming something of a cause célèbre on the continent. A military court martial sentenced him to life imprisonment. Lee had taken just the incident of the assassination attempt and the fact that he was a poet, and had written her play without knowing any other facts. She wanted to tell the story of a hero in a world that seemed, at present, to be bereft of heroic figures.

There was a large cast with only two parts for women. The morning was spent just auditioning actors, and Paul had chosen the scene where Alekos tried to convince his best friend, Heracles, to aid him in the assassination. Frank read the part of Heracles onstage while a steady stream of actors tried out by reading the part of Alekos.

Lee was surprised by the quality of the readings; it seemed like the best young actors in New York had all turned up for the audition. She made notes next to the names of several; while they might not be what she had in mind for Alekos, there were several smaller roles for men and she saw they'd have no difficulty in filling them. One young man, Dan Roentch, gave a particularly fine reading, and Lee nudged Paul at its conclusion.

"He's got a matter-of-fact quality that would be perfect for Heracles."

"Yes, I was thinking the same thing," Paul agreed.

Paul called up to Frank to read the part of Alekos to Dan's Heracles, and when they had finished, Paul and Lee looked at each other and nodded. The part of Heracles was second in importance only to Alekos, and they both felt gratified to have filled it so easily.

"I take it you're available, Dan," Paul called up to the actor. "No movie commitments? TV?"

36

Dan grinned down at them. "I'd get out of them for a chance to work with you again, Paul."

"Is he being sarcastic?" Lee whispered to Paul, knowing how much more money actors made from movies than from the stage.

Paul looked insulted. "Don't judge everyone by yourself; some people sincerely mean what they say," he said, matching her own sarcasm, and Lee couldn't stop herself from laughing out loud.

Frank heard the laughter and called down to them. "How about a short break? I've been reading for almost two hours."

"Sure, if you'll bring us some coffee," Paul agreed. "Lee can't seem to manage it without spilling."

Frank brought them each another cup of coffee plus a bag containing two jelly donuts, which he handed to Lee. Paul spotted them and had one in his hand before Lee could stop him.

"Hey, those are for me," she protested.

"I didn't have any breakfast." Paul already had half of it in his mouth.

"That's your fault—*I* would have liked some," said Lee, thinking one lone donut wasn't going to quell the rumbling in her stomach.

"I forgot about it," Paul said, eyeing the uneaten portion of her donut with an expression bordering on lust. Lee quickly finished it and they spent the rest of the break discussing some of the actors they had seen. Paul suggested two or three as having the ability to carry the part of Alekos, but Lee felt they lacked a certain quality that she wanted the hero to possess.

The second actor to try out after the break was Richard Jesse, and Lee caught her breath as he came on to read. He had a presence, a quality about him that seemed to light up the stage, and his looks were breathtaking. Exactly the way she had always pictured Alekos. It was as if he had come back to life and was standing on the stage, reading to her.

During the morning Paul had asked some of the actors to come back the next day for a second reading. When Richard had finished, Lee waited for Paul to ask the actor to return. He remained silent.

"Ask him to come back," she whispered to him.

"No, Lee," Paul started to say, but Lee wasn't about to have her Alekos disappear.

"Frank," she called up to the stage, "have Mr. Jesse return tomorrow for a second reading."

Richard shaded his eyes, peered down at her, then turned to Frank and conferred with him. Frank was laughing when Richard, turning for one last look at Lee, left the stage.

"What was that all about, Frank?" Paul's voice boomed out.

Frank was still enjoying the joke. "He thought Lee was your secretary," Frank explained. "Couldn't seem to believe it when I said she was the playwright."

Paul turned cold eyes on Lee. "Please don't override me again."

"Don't I have a say in the casting?" Lee asked him in an innocent voice, knowing full well she had.

"*I'm* the one who's going to have to work with the actors."

She was equally as adamant. "And it's *my* play they're going to be doing."

"We'll discuss it later," he said dismissively.

"That's fine with me," Lee muttered to herself, wondering when they were going to have lunch, as she was starved.

An hour later they finally broke for lunch. Instead of leaving the theater, though, as Lee had anticipated, Paul asked Frank to order some sandwiches, as he and Lee would be eating in his office.

She followed him to a small room as neat and uncluttered as his living room was the opposite. "It doesn't look like you ever use it."

"I don't. Sit down and let's talk." He was behind the desk in the one comfortable seat. She pulled a wooden folding chair up and sat across from him.

"I'd rather eat first."

"So would I, but we don't have any time to waste." He lighted what must be his fiftieth cigarette of the day. "What's with your mania for Jesse?"

"I want him for Alekos."

"Was he coming on to you earlier? Is that it? Listen, Lee, you're going to have to get used to the fact actors try to butter up playwrights. It's a whole way of life in the theater; actors will go to any length to get a part."

"Give me credit for knowing when I'm being buttered up. I teach school; students aren't any different. Anyway, he thought I was an actress at first and after that, when he saw me out front, he assumed I was your secretary."

Paul looked doubtful. "So he says."

"You didn't believe I was the playwright when you met me. You really believe Richard Jesse thought the Village Playhouse was suddenly producing a woman's play? Or maybe you think he's psychic."

He looked annoyed. "Okay, so you felt an instant attraction for the guy. Go out with him, but keep him out of the play."

"The instant attraction was because it was like meeting Alekos in person. He's perfect for the part." Lee didn't actually remember thinking any such thing when she first saw Richard.

"He's too young."

"He looks like he's in his twenties," Lee argued.

"Early twenties. Alekos was twenty-eight."

"Which seems a little old for a student. Anyway, I wrote a fictionalized version and I think I prefer him to be younger."

Frank came in with a plate piled high with sandwiches

and a half dozen Cokes. Lee decided to get a second opinion. "What do you think of Richard Jesse playing Alekos, Frank?" she asked him.

Frank winked at her. "Personally, I think *I'm* perfect for the role."

"You have red hair."

"I'd be willing to dye it."

"Forget it, Frank," Paul broke in. "It's easier to find actors than business managers. But if you're interested, you can understudy the part of Heracles."

Lee wanted to ask Frank again what he thought of the young actor, but by then her mouth was full of sandwich and by the time she swallowed it, he had left. She quickly took one more bite before continuing the argument.

"Will you at least keep an open mind about him when he reads tomorrow?"

Paul glared at her. "I always keep an open mind."

"Sure, that's why you didn't want to work with a woman playwright," she reminded him.

"I'm working with you, aren't I?"

They spent the rest of the time discussing the different actors they had seen. Surprisingly enough, they were in complete agreement about most of them. Lee was hopeful that with a little persuasion she could talk Paul into giving Richard Jesse the part.

The afternoon was devoted to auditioning actresses for the two female roles. One role was that of Athena, Heracles's girl friend, who sees her father being tortured and killed by Papadopoulos's men. It was a small part but called for a sensitive actress who could do the monologue without making it sound maudlin. The other role was that of Dora, the most militant member of the underground and Alekos's former sweetheart. It was a pivotal role, that of the antagonist, and Lee was going to be very particular about how it was cast.

Midway through the readings, a lovely young woman came on stage and gave a fine audition. Lee didn't think her right for the part of Dora, but the actress had the same quality of lighting up the stage that Richard Jesse possessed. Without conferring with Lee, Paul asked her to return the following day, then called for a fifteen-minute break.

"Who do you have her in mind for?" Lee asked him. "Athena?"

"No. Dora."

"That's not how *I* envision Dora," she told him.

"Listen, directors envision actors in parts when they read a play too, you know."

"She's just not the type."

"I'm the one who's going to have to work with her, and she's easy to work with."

Lee gave him a disbelieving look. "Easy to look at, you mean."

"Christie? I hadn't noticed."

"You just practically fell out of your seat when she walked on stage."

Paul looked affronted. "You've got to be kidding. Listen, this is strictly business. I'm around actresses all the time; all I care about is whether or not they can act. How they look isn't that important. This is a play, you know, not a movie. There aren't going to be any close-ups."

Something annoyingly like a feeling of jealousy came over Lee as she listened to him. He even remembered the girl's name. "She looks like a high-school cheerleader. An *aging* high-school cheerleader."

He looked perplexed. "So what's wrong with that?"

"Dora would never have been a cheerleader."

"Come on, she wasn't always a militant."

"Alekos wouldn't have liked that type."

Paul stared at her in disbelief. "You're telling me a Greek wouldn't appreciate a beautiful girl?"

Lee felt unreasonably incensed. "See? It *is* her looks you're impressed with."

41

"Yeah, Lee? Well, just what was it about Jesse that impressed you so much?"

"He looks Greek. He's a good actor. He's got a wonderful voice. He's perfect—exactly how I pictured Alekos. Better, in fact."

"Don't give me any of that nonsense about his acting ability or his voice. You like his looks—period!"

"Yes," Lee admitted, "but if he couldn't act I wouldn't want him in my play no matter how good he looked." She turned away from him. "Christie! She looks like a Christie!"

"And *you*, my dear, look like a Merrilee," he retorted, effectively silencing her for the moment.

Lee slouched down in her seat for the rest of the auditions, uncomfortably aware of Paul's nearness. He was a rude, opinionated, thoroughly unlikable man. And yet, despite Richard Jesse's looks and friendly manner, he didn't appeal to her in the same way Paul did. She had felt a very strong physical attraction for Paul from the first; an attraction that only seemed heightened whenever they clashed, which has got to be a perversity, Lee thought to herself. She had lain awake a long time the night before, very aware of Paul's presence in the room below hers. It was odd, she thought, but she was sure she'd have had no trouble getting to sleep if it had been Richard Jesse below.

The seemingly endless auditions were finally over for the day and Lee followed Paul out of the theater. She blinked in the strong sunlight. It seemed like it should have been the middle of the night, but it was only seven o'clock.

"Where do you want to eat?" Paul asked her.

"Somewhere with American food," she informed him.

"What a waste," muttered Paul, but led her over to Shakespeare's on Macdougal Street, where Lee happily consumed a steak, baked potato, and salad.

"Do we watch the ballgame tonight?" she inquired over dessert.

"No, we've goofed off enough. We really need to discuss act one tonight so you can get started on the revisions before we go into rehearsals."

Lee felt stung. "I *like* act one—it's act two I had all the difficulty with."

"Exactly. That's why we'll start with the easiest one."

A truly insufferable man, Lee acknowledged to herself. She couldn't for the life of her figure out his appeal. But there was no doubt he did appeal to her.

CHAPTER FOUR

"I don't see why he has to have weaknesses." Lee was shouting, something she normally never indulged in, but Paul invariably brought out the worst in her. They had been arguing about this one point for hours and seemed to be getting nowhere.

"Can't you get it through that thick skull of yours that it makes him more interesting?"

"To whom?" Lee liked Alekos just the way she had written him.

"To the audience. To the critics. To *me!* If you ever learned anything at all about playwriting, you know the protagonist has to have conflicts."

Lee stubbornly maintained her position. "He's in conflict with the other members of the Resistance. He's in conflict with the state. There is no reason why he has to be in conflict with himself too."

Paul stood over her where she was sprawled out on the couch in his den. "You know something, Masterson? You have a tenacity that borders on . . . blockheadedness!"

Lee repeated to herself what he had just said, then burst out laughing. " 'A tenacity that borders on blockheadedness,' I love it! Can I use that line in my new play, Paul?" Her laughter had eased the tension.

"Be my guest. You're working on a new play?"

Lee nodded. "The first draft is done; I'm working on the revisions now."

He pushed her feet, that were beside her on the couch, over and sat down next to her. "When do I get to read it?"

"I didn't think you'd be interested."

"I'm always interested in reading new plays."

"This one's not political—it's more of a comedy."

His interest faded somewhat. "I'd still like to see it. What's it about?"

"It's a two-character play. A young man and a young woman."

"I asked what it was *about*."

Lee thought a moment. "Freedom. I always seem to write about freedom."

"Tell me. In your new play do your characters have conflicts within themselves?"

"Of course—and with each other."

"What, exactly, is your hang-up regarding Alekos?" He eyed her thoughtfully. "Do you demand that a man be perfect?"

Lee thought for a moment. "I think a hero should be perfect."

"A hero is a man. But, hell, even the Greek gods weren't perfect."

"I think Alekos was perfect," Lee said softly.

"It would really bother you for him to have some faults, wouldn't it?"

She nodded.

He shook his head. "Look, Lee, I'm not saying that you couldn't conceivably be right and me wrong. Maybe Alekos didn't have any inner conflicts about assassinating Papadopoulos, although I find that hard to believe. But even if he didn't in real life, he has to in a play or it just doesn't work dramatically. Even Hamlet had inner conflicts, and he's the greatest tragic hero we have in the theater."

"I don't care," Lee said, her voice sounding a little shaky. "I want him to be perfect."

Paul lighted a cigarette and seemed to be pondering her

last remark. "You're in love with him, aren't you? In love with Alexandros Panagoulis."

"Don't be ridiculous—he's dead." But a shiver had run through her at his perceptive statement.

"You're in love with his memory."

"Perhaps," she admitted. "Is that wrong?" She recalled how when writing the play she had become totally immersed in the young Greek's story to the exclusion of everything else. She hadn't even dated during the months she spent writing it; no man could live up to the image she carried with her of Alekos.

"Yes, I think it's wrong. Oh, not from a romantic point of view—if you want to be in love with a dead man, go right ahead. I know some people go in for unrequited love in a big way. But from a playwright's point of view it's dangerous. It's clouded your ability to be objective."

Lee gave him a wry smile. "Perhaps you're right. Yes, I suspect you are. My department head read it and said the same thing. All right, what faults should I give him? What conflicts?"

"That's for you to decide. You're the playwright."

Lee stood up and stretched. "I'll just select a couple of *your* faults, then," she told Paul with a grin, making her exit before he could come back with a suitable retort. But his laughter followed her as she went upstairs to bed.

She stayed up late, alternately working on her revisions and thinking of Paul. It was not Alekos but Paul she dreamed of that night. He was yelling at her about something, his smile mocking, the gleam in his eyes canceling out the anger. She slept restlessly, waking up several times during the night.

She woke up early the next morning and felt she had probably adjusted to New York time.

She dressed in white cotton pants, a red-and-white striped T-shirt, and her running shoes. She let herself quietly out of the apartment, careful not to wake Paul. She had noticed a delicatessen at the corner of his block and went inside to purchase the ingredients for breakfast. She was no gourmet cook, but she could manage bacon and eggs.

She was setting the food out on the table when Paul appeared. His rumpled look disarmed her. "Good morning, did you sleep well?" she asked him.

He blinked at such early morning cheer. "Umm—how about you, get any work done last night?"

"Quite a bit. I'd show it to you, but you'd never be able to decipher my writing. Is there a typewriter at the theater I can use?"

"Sure." He eyed the food. "Is some of this for me?"

"Of course."

"Well, keep the receipt. We'll reimburse you."

Lee smiled at him. "I don't mind buying you breakfast occasionally."

He looked surprised. "What's with you? You're being awfully pleasant all of a sudden."

"I'm always pleasant around congenial people. I just don't usually happen to find you congenial."

He grinned. "Hey, that's more like it. Now I recognize you." He started in on the food. "So, tell me about your revisions. What inner conflict did you give Alekos?"

"I made him a pacifist."

He gave a low whistle. "Beautiful, just beautiful. Yeah, I like it—it'll play." He waited for her to go on, and when she didn't, he said, "Well, go on, what faults did you give him?"

Lee swallowed and averted her eyes. "I decided to make him impotent."

There was a silence. "Come again?"

With an effort she met his eyes. "I made him impotent. You know . . ."

"I *know* what the word means. Can you elaborate on that?"

Lee searched for the right words. "I tried to think what would really bother a Greek man. . . ."

48

"That would bother *any* man," Paul muttered.

"Yes, well, *especially* a Greek man."

"I don't know about that."

"Well *I* do. They're very macho over there."

"Some of us can be—"

"Don't confuse macho with obnoxious," Lee broke in, momentarily disconcerting Paul to the point where he let her talk on without interruption.

"I think it's valid," she went on. "I believe that loss of freedom to him—particularly the freedom to write what he wanted—might have that effect on him. I've read about wild animals becoming impotent while they're in captivity, and I think the same thing could happen to Alekos. But the thing that would be the most important to him, Paul, wouldn't be his . . . sexual impotence. It would be the fact that he had become impotent creatively as well. He couldn't write poems anymore." She paused and waited anxiously for his opinion.

His smile warmed her. "I've got to admit, Masterson, I think it's brilliant."

"Honest?"

"Honest. My girl, we're going to have ourselves a play!"

She got up from the table, feeling good enough to do a dance around the room. "Better start cleaning up, Paul. We have to leave soon."

He choked on his coffee. "You expect *me* to do the dishes?"

"When I cook, you clean up," she informed him, and congratulated herself on two brilliant exit lines in a row. But the congratulations were premature.

"I've got a cleaning woman," he yelled after her. "*She* can do the dishes."

CHAPTER FIVE

The first part of the call-backs went smoothly. With Dan Roentch reading the part of Heracles, a half dozen young actresses read the part of Athena. The girl had only one scene in the play, but it consisted of a long monologue wherein she related having seen her father tortured and killed. It could be a real tear-jerker, but that wasn't the way Lee wanted it done. It was only one in a series of atrocities committed by the Colonels, and Lee didn't want it to assume more importance than any of the others.

There was one young actress, Nonie Pratt, whom Lee particularly liked. The girl was tiny, but with a toughness about her, and her voice had a hoarse quality that was appealing.

"I really like her," she whispered to Paul when the actress had read for the second time that morning. "What do you think?"

Paul nodded. "I hesitated before because I've never seen her work, but I think I'm inclined to agree with you."

He called up to the stage. "Miss Pratt, did you bring a resume with you?"

A smile appeared on the young woman's face. "Yes, would you like to see it?"

"Why don't you bring it down here for a moment?" Paul suggested.

Nonie came off the stage and sat in the row ahead of them. She turned around in her seat while Paul glanced over her credits.

"You're not Equity, I see," he murmured, and the girl looked crestfallen.

"No; no, I'm not."

He looked up at her with a grin. "Well, you will be now."

"Oh, thank you," said Nonie, tears coming to her eyes.

Paul looked over at Lee. "It was a joint decision. This is the playwright, Lee Masterson."

Nonie held out her hand and Lee took it, not sure she liked the power she had suddenly assumed over young actors' futures.

"Rehearsals start Monday," Paul told Nonie. "Talk to Frank about getting fixed up with Equity."

When the girl had left, Lee turned to Paul. "I would have felt terrible if you had turned her down after getting her hopes up."

"You'll become hardened after a while. You can't make them all stars, and unfortunately it's not always the sweet ones like her you give the jobs to. Hell, Lee, we're not do-gooders here. It's the success of the play we've got to be concerned with."

By lunchtime they still were not in agreement over the parts of Alekos and Dora. Lee was still holding firm for Richard Jesse; Paul was equally adamant about Christie Sumner. Paul was about to call a lunch break when Lee grabbed hold of his arm.

"Wait a minute, Paul. If we can't resolve it now, eating lunch isn't going to help."

"It'll help the condition of my stomach," Paul muttered.

"Seriously, I think we should try something new. Why don't we have Richard and Christie do a scene together— see how they play together. Who knows, they might be disastrous!"

Paul considered her suggestion for a moment. "Why not? What have we got to lose?"

"Frank," he called up to the stage, "get Jesse and Sumner back out. Tell them to read scene three from the top."

The two actors gave a good cold reading of the unfamiliar lines. At the end of it Lee turned to Paul. "Well, at least I see they're all wrong together."

"What do you mean?"

"That girl is at least four inches taller than Richard."

"I know. I found that interesting."

"*Interesting?*" Lee sounded incredulous.

"Yeah, I like offbeat casting. Listen, do you know what's beautiful about it?"

Lee shook her head.

"It tells a lot about Alekos. Only a really together, self-confident type of guy would go with a girl who was taller than him. Yeah, I like it; I really do."

Lee thought about it for a moment and saw his point. To be honest, what she objected to was that girl making her hero look so short. But Richard had such stage presence it probably wouldn't matter. She also knew her best chance of getting Paul to go along with casting Richard Jesse would be for her to go along with Christie Sumner.

"Yes, I think you're right," she said to him. "That *is* interesting casting."

Paul chuckled. "Don't think I don't know how that devious mind of yours is working. You're thinking, *Give the director Christie Sumner and I'll get my Alekos.* Am I right?"

Lee grinned. "We can discuss it at lunch."

"No need to discuss anything. Is it a deal?" He held out his hand.

Lee shook it. "It's a deal."

"Looks as though you two got yourselves the parts," he called up to the actors. "Rehearsals start Monday 10:00 A.M. sharp."

There were shouts of joy from the stage as Paul grabbed Lee's hand and dragged her up the aisle. "Come on, we've got the afternoon off. I'm going to take you down to Chinatown for Szechuan."

"For *what?*"

"Never had it? Boy, are you in for a treat."

The Szechuan was not an unqualified success as far as Paul was concerned. Anticipating howls of pain over the highly seasoned food, he was sorely disappointed. Lee, a Californian brought up on Mexican food, merely pronounced it "tasty," and drank only one glass of water to his three.

Paul walked her home from Chinatown through Soho and Little Italy, and they browsed in some of the shops and galleries along the way.

"Listen," he said to her as they entered his brownstone, "I'm supposed to go to a party tonight. You want to come along?"

"Sure."

"It's at Harry Duke's place," he said, mentioning the name of one of Broadway's most famous producers. "It'll be mostly theater people, probably pretty boring."

Lee gave him an indignant look. "Boring to you, maybe, not to me. I think it'll be exciting to meet people I've only read about. I'm fascinated by the theater." She paused. "I also don't have anything to wear."

He shrugged. "Jeans are okay. Nobody dresses up at these things. Anyway, even if they did, you're a writer. Writers are allowed to be eccentric."

Lee looked at her watch; it was only four o'clock. "What are you going to do now?"

"I've got some work to do."

Lee looked at him suspiciously. "Does that mean there's a ballgame on?"

"No, it means I have some work to do. Why don't you go over to the theater and type up your revisions?"

"Are you trying to get rid of me?"

He gave her a look of exasperation. "What are you doing, becoming paranoid? You think this is some deep

54

plot to get you out of my house so I can watch a ballgame alone?"

"I don't feel like typing up my revisions. I have all weekend to do that. What are *you* going to do?"

"That's none of your business! Well, actually I was thinking of taking a nap."

"You take naps?"

He looked as though he'd like to kick her. "No, I don't take naps! It's just that I haven't been sleeping very well on the couch."

Lee instantly felt guilty. "But you told me you fell asleep on it all the time."

He nodded. "Sure, when I'm watching TV I always fall asleep on it. But now, when I'm *trying* to sleep on it, I can't seem to go to sleep."

"Maybe you should keep the TV on," Lee suggested.

"Yeah, maybe you're right."

Lee still felt guilty. "Listen, you're right. I should get those revisions typed up. What time's the party?"

"Around ten."

"Why don't you go upstairs and get some sleep on the bed while I go over to the theater. I'll wake you up about nine. Okay?"

"You're beginning to sound like my mother." He teased her, then retreated up the stairs before she could think of a suitable retort.

As soon as she heard him collapse on the bed, she remembered the revisions were in the bedroom. She found the morning paper on the hall table and went into the den to read it. She settled down on the couch and found that she had no trouble at all falling asleep on it.

Lee woke up to darkness. She switched on the lamp and glanced at her watch. It was ten thirty. She went upstairs, switching on lights along the way. She turned on the overhead light in the bedroom. "Hey, wake up, you overslept."

His eyes slowly opened and regarded her thoughtfully. "What did you say?"

"I said you overslept. It's ten thirty."

"If I recall, you were going to wake me at nine."

"Well, *I* overslept."

"Where were *you* sleeping?"

"On the couch. My revisions were in here and I didn't want to disturb you."

His eyes gleamed. "I would have loved to have you disturb me."

Lee went over to the closet and opened it. "You can get out of here now so I can get ready."

"Yes, ma'am. How long's it going to take you?"

"Ten minutes. How long's it going to take you?"

"Longer than that," he admitted, looking impressed.

Lee took a quick shower, fastened her hair back from her face with combs, and dressed in designer jeans, a beige silk shirt, and her high-heeled sandals. She was downstairs in less than ten minutes and fixing herself a scrambled-egg sandwich when Paul appeared in the kitchen.

"There'll be food at the party," he informed her.

"I want something now."

He sat down at the table. "You had a huge lunch."

"That was hours ago." She brought her sandwich over to the table and sat down.

"Can I have half?"

"Sure." She picked up her half and pushed the plate in front of him.

"It would be good with some coffee."

"Then fix some."

"But I don't really need it."

Lee wondered how he kept himself fed before her arrival.

CHAPTER SIX

Over Lee's protests, they took a taxi to the party. She was still eager to ride on a subway, but Paul told her it wouldn't be with him.

"If you want to get yourself killed, you do it without me," he had told her as he flagged down a cab.

"Coward," Lee had muttered under her breath, but if Paul overheard her remark he didn't comment on it. Which meant, she was certain, he hadn't heard it.

During the drive Paul told her that Harry Duke lived on the Upper West Side.

"The upper west side of what?"

"Of Manhattan. On Central Park West, actually. Wait'll you see the view of the park from his terrace."

"What I'd like to see," Lee told him, "is the park itself. I understand it has a zoo."

"So I've heard." Paul sounded disinterested.

"You've never been there?"

Paul shook his head.

"Would you show it to me?"

"No way! Stay out of Central Park. It's dangerous!"

Lee looked puzzled. "I've heard they have concerts and opera and Shakespeare and a lot of other things there. It couldn't be all that dangerous."

"Take my word for it."

"I don't understand you, Paul. You won't take a subway, you won't go to Central Park. How can you stand living in New York if you're afraid to go anywhere?"

"I'm not afraid, I'm just cautious. Anyway, there's a lot more to this city than subways and Central Park."

Lee gave up the argument and stared out the window. She was wondering how she could be physically attracted to a coward. One thing was for sure—Paul could never be a hero. Heroes weren't afraid of anything. "Alekos wouldn't be afraid to ride a subway."

She hadn't realized she had spoken aloud until she saw his amused look.

"Yeah, and he ended up dead at a very early age too."

"But not from a subway ride."

"So all that proves is I'm not a hero. Right?"

Lee ignored him.

"Am I right?"

"Absolutely."

"I never said I was a hero."

The driver pulled up in front of a very old building and they got out. Lee stood for a moment looking up at it.

"I thought a big producer like Duke would be rich."

"He is," Paul assured her.

"And he lives in this old building?"

"This is the Dakota," he explained to her patiently.

"A building like this in California would be considered a slum."

"Lauren Bacall lives here."

"Oh, come on! In *this* building?"

"I'm serious. She might even be at the party."

He took her hand and managed to get her inside. The elevator was unlike anything Lee had ever ridden in. She was sure it should be condemned and wondered how someone as cowardly as Paul had the guts to ride in it.

The apartment, however, she found a pleasant surprise. Even though it was filled wall-to-wall with people, she could see how beautifully the spacious rooms were decorated. She spotted waiters walking around wearing white coats and carrying trays of drinks and, in one corner, a man in a tuxedo was seated at a piano playing show tunes.

The rest of the people were, as Paul had advised her, dressed very casually.

Paul introduced her to their host, Harry Duke, a balding, affable man in his late fifties.

"This is the Playhouse's new discovery, Harry. She's written our season's first production."

Harry Duke smiled broadly. "I'm glad to see you people down there have finally discovered there are two sexes."

"They thought I was a man," Lee told him candidly.

Harry laughed out loud. "Then they must be blind." He put a hand on Paul's shoulder. "Something I might be interested in taking to Broadway, Paul?"

Paul shook his head. "No, it's not a musical."

"I've been known to produce other things," Harry persisted.

"It's not a comedy either."

Harry smiled at Lee. "Well, the best of luck with it anyway, young lady. Maybe if you ever turn it into a musical . . ."

Lee tried to imagine *Alekos* as a musical and failed.

Paul turned to Lee. "Listen, get yourself a drink and take a look at the view from the terrace. I've got to talk some business with a few people." He disappeared into the crowd without waiting for an answer.

My hero, thought Lee. *Takes me to a party where I don't know a soul, and then deserts me.* She looked around for a waiter and got herself a glass of champagne, then moved in the direction of the piano where a crowd of young men was gathered about singing the score from *A Chorus Line.* Lee had been to parties before where the guests had sung, but never guests with such talent. It occurred to her that they could very well be professionals and had probably sung the songs on stage in Harry's musicals. She would have liked to join in but was afraid her voice would create the one disparate note.

There was a good number of women at the party, but the men outnumbered them by about four to one. Which wasn't bad odds, Lee thought, as her eyes surveyed more good-looking men than she had ever seen gathered in one room before.

What seemed strange to her, though, was that very few of the men seemed to be paying any attention to the women. They were clustered in groups, all seemingly very good friends. The ones around the piano even had their arms around each other's shoulders. Like a group of college boys in a fraternity house. Or like . . .

Lee blushed with the realization of how naive she had been. Well, she should have known. She wasn't the best-looking woman at the party by any means, not with all the actresses present, but it was odd that none of the men had even looked at her twice. She shook her head at her own stupidity and moved off to find the terrace.

Before she could find it, something more interesting caught her eye. A buffet—the proportions of which staggered her. A more awesome display of food she had never seen. She was quickly filling up her plate when she heard a low chuckle behind her and turned to see John Melfi.

He smiled at her. "You don't know how refreshing it is to see someone in New York who's not on a perpetual diet."

"I haven't had any dinner," Lee explained.

"Isn't Paul feeding you?"

"Oh, yes, but we slept through dinner." She saw his startled look and realized how that had sounded. "I mean Paul was tired and was taking a nap and I was supposed to wake him in time for the party, but I fell asleep on the couch and . . ."

"You don't have to explain," he assured her. "I didn't think you were sleeping together. I consider it a miracle you're even speaking to each other after that inauspicious start you got off to."

"He's been pretty nice actually," Lee told him. "Except for some disagreements over casting, we've been getting along fine."

"I hear you finished casting this noon. Are you happy with it?"

Lee nodded. "There's one person I have my doubts about, but all in all I think it's an excellent cast."

"If you have doubts only about one, you're doing fine."

Lee had been piling food on her plate as they talked and she now saw it was close to overflowing. John's plate ran a close second; they seemed to be the only two at the party eating.

John looked around. "Would you like to sit down at a table out on the terrace?"

"I'd love to. Paul told me to be sure and see the view."

She followed him through two rooms and then out French doors to a terrace that was at least fifteen feet wide and the entire length of the apartment. They found a vacant table at the far end, complete with linen tablecloth and a candle, and were seated.

Lee looked out over the park but couldn't see much in the darkness.

"It's better in the daytime," John said, as though reading her thoughts. "But at least you're not looking into someone else's windows at night, which is the view most of us have. That or a brick wall."

Lee thought of her own view of the ocean at home and wasn't unduly impressed.

She spent an interesting hour or so talking to John. He told her the whole history of the Village Playhouse: how it was founded, what playwrights they had discovered, and the backgrounds of some of the members. He didn't say anything about Paul's background, and Lee longed to ask him, but was afraid of sounding personally interested in the man.

When he finally excused himself, saying he wanted to make an early night of it, Lee went in search of Paul.

It didn't take her long to find him. He was standing by the buffet talking to a young man with a cloud of blond curls and an angelic face. He was laughing at something

61

the boy was telling him, looking more animated than he ever looked when he was with her. And for someone who loved food as much as he did, he hadn't even filled a plate.

Lee was about to interrupt them and, at the same time, help herself to some more food, when Paul put his hand on the young man's arm and bent over the blond head, saying something so softly she couldn't hear.

Lee froze. How could I have been so stupid, she thought with chagrin. No wonder he hadn't cared to work with a woman playwright. No wonder she had felt so safe staying alone with him in his apartment. And no wonder the physical attraction she felt for him was so one-sided. What was it he had said to her about her feelings for Alekos? Something about certain people going in for unrequited love? Well, she had done it again. First a dead hero, now a man who preferred men.

Lee lost her desire for any more food; what she needed was a drink. She went over to the bar set up in one corner of the living room and requested a vodka martini. She drank it down quickly and the bartender set a second one in front of her without being asked.

Lee knew that her capacity for alcohol was not great, so she picked up the second drink and looked around for a place to sit down. There was no place available in the living room, but wandering down the hall she spotted a small, book-lined study that was empty, and she went inside and seated herself comfortably in a leather recliner.

She drank her second martini slowly, thinking about what she had discovered. It occurred to her that she might have a problem that required the services of an analyst. Perhaps she was drawn only to men whom she couldn't have. Was that why she was still unmarried at twenty-eight? She was sure her mother would tell her that was the case, but then her mother felt the only state to be in was a married state. She remembered her mother's advice to her when Lee had been embarking upon her master's degree. Something about how too much education would

scare off the men. Well, the only man she had been seriously interested in had had several more degrees than she; the
only thing that had eventually scared him off was the fact
that he was married to the dean's daughter and Lee was
one of his students.

"No, I don't believe it!" she spoke aloud.

"You don't believe what?"

The voice came from a darkened corner of the room.
Lee looked over and could make out the barely discernible
form of a man sprawled out on a couch.

"I was thinking that there was an innate flaw in me, but
upon careful consideration, I just don't believe it."

"I should think not!" His voice was low with the trace
of an accent. "Of course I'm only going by your outward
appearance, but I don't perceive any flaws there."

A compliment. From a man. At *this* party. Lee wondered if she had beaten the odds. Probably not. If he were
really available, he'd no doubt be surrounded by women.

"Thank you for saying that. My ego has not exactly
been enhanced by this party."

"What did you expect at one of Duke's parties? Every
chorus boy who ever worked for him is here—most of
them hoping to land a part in his new musical."

"But I thought Duke was married."

He laughed. "What part of Iowa did you say you were
from?"

"Very funny," said Lee without humor. "I'm from California and we're not that naive out there. Of course I'm
from southern California, not San Francisco." Lee started
to chuckle.

"You're amused too, I see."

"I was just thinking," said Lee. "This would make a
funny scene in a play."

"Oh, God, not another playwright!" The man got off
the couch and walked over to get a closer look at Lee.
"You here to interest Duke in your work?"

Lee looked up at him and got an impression of a lot of

hair: a bushy mop of black curls, an equally bushy mustache, and a full beard. "No, I'm here with Paul Devon."

"You're kidding!" The man seemed startled and Lee realized she was probably the only one at the party who hadn't known of Paul's affinity for men.

"It's not a date," she explained to him coolly. "He's directing my play, I'm currently his houseguest, and he brought me along because he didn't know what else to do with me, I guess."

The man grinned. "*I'd* know what else to do with you."

Lee ignored that remark.

"Can I get you another drink?"

Lee handed him her glass. "You certainly may. I feel like really getting smashed tonight. A vodka martini, please."

He was back shortly with drinks for both of them and took a seat opposite her. "I'm Gene Lesnek," he introduced himself, offering her a cigarette.

She had given up smoking two years before, but suddenly felt an overwhelming urge to have one and gave in to the urge.

"Lee Masterson," she said. He was looking at her peculiarly, almost in disbelief. "That's my name—really. Well, actually it's Merrilee, but I prefer Lee." He was still staring at her. "What's the matter? I can't believe you've heard of me already; I've only been here a few days."

"No, no," he shook his head. "It was just that you didn't seem to recognize *my* name."

Lee thought quickly, but couldn't remember ever hearing the name Gene Lesnek before. "I'm sorry, should I have heard of you? I've really committed a blunder, right? Should I be asking for your autograph?"

"No, I wouldn't think so."

Given the circumstances of who was giving the party, Lee made a guess. "If you're a musical-comedy star, I probably wouldn't have heard of you unless you made the movie version."

"Do I look like a musical-comedy star?"

"Well, no . . ." Lee stared at him, certain she would know if she had ever seen him before. If nothing else, she'd remember all the hair. "I don't watch TV much, except for sports."

"Neither do I. Watch TV, that is. I don't care for sports."

"You might as well tell me who you are," Lee said. "You could be the mayor of New York as far as I know; I'm just not that familiar with the city."

"There's no reason why you should have heard of me, not being a New Yorker. I'm a newspaper reporter of sorts, that's all. But tell me about your play. Is it a romantic comedy?"

"Actually, it's a Greek tragedy."

"*What?*"

Lee laughed. "A modern Greek tragedy. It's about Alexandros Panagoulis. Being a reporter, you may have heard of him."

"I remember his trial well. I'm surprised. You don't look like the writer of a political play."

"You sound like Paul. It's not a political play. And *you* don't look like a reporter."

He scratched his beard. "What do I look like?"

"A sixties radical."

His laugh boomed out. "I was, in a way. But not in this country. Tell me about your play; the subject matter fascinates me."

Lee told him about *Alekos* in detail. Then, later, they discussed Greece under the Colonels, a subject in which he was quite knowledgeable. He occasionally went out and refilled their drinks. The last time he returned he told her Paul was looking for her.

"Do you want me to tell him where you are? I think he wants to go home."

"I guess so," said Lee, not anxious to see Paul. She was afraid she'd act ill at ease around him now.

65

"I'd be glad to take you home if you want to stay longer."

Lee smiled up at him. "Thanks, but I better go with Paul."

Gene was about to leave, then turned back. "May I ask you something?"

"Sure."

"I know you're busy now with the play going into rehearsals, but would it be all right to call you after it opens? We could have dinner—continue our discussion."

"I'd like that," Lee told him, thinking what a nice man he was. Also intelligent. Not bad looking either.

When Paul appeared in the doorway a few minutes later, Lee got to her feet. She suddenly felt the effects of all the vodka and put a hand on the chair to steady herself.

"Can't I leave you alone at a party without your getting drunk, Masterson?"

"I'm not drunk," Lee informed him. "I can speak perfectly coherently, I just can't perambulate so well."

"Yeah, you writers all talk good when you're drunk. But you're still drunk." He took her arm. "Come on, let's get out of here."

She noticed his words were slurred. "You're as drunk as I am."

"That's okay, I'm not driving."

"True," she agreed.

She didn't remember much of the drive home, having dozed off in the taxi, but she felt a little more sober when she got out of the cab and had no trouble navigating to the brownstone. They were no sooner inside with the door closed when Paul put his arms around her and kissed her. She was just about to respond when memories of the party came back to her. She shoved him away. "What do you think you're doing?"

"I thought I was kissing you." He leaned back against the door.

"Exactly! You must really be drunk to be kissing *me*."

"It did help," he admitted.

"You can just forget the macho display—I know about you."

"You know about me?"

Lee nodded, envying him the door he was leaning against. But then if she leaned against something, she was sure she would fall asleep.

"I'm trying to figure out what you know about me, but my mind isn't functioning too well."

"Look, I *know*. I saw you at the party with the blond. The blond young man. I guess I'm a little . . . uh . . . slow."

Paul appeared confused for a moment, then an incredulous look passed over his face. "Are you intimating that I'm gay? Me? You're not slow, you're deranged!"

Lee took a step back, almost losing her balance. "But you and he . . . you looked like . . . and everyone else seemed to be . . ." She shook her head, trying to clear it.

"That 'blond' just happens to be one of the best set designers around. And I got him to agree to do *Alekos*. I told you I was there to talk business."

"But isn't he . . . ?"

"Gay? Sure he is. Does that matter?"

"Of course not. Not at all. Why should it matter?" Lee babbled, suddenly realizing Paul had actually kissed her and that he liked women. And she had probably blown it and now he'd never kiss her again.

"I didn't think I appealed to you," she said.

"Are you crazy?" he yelled. "Why the hell do you think I've been getting no sleep? It's been because the thought of you upstairs in *my* bedroom, sleeping in *my* bed, was driving me nuts!"

Lee thought the conversation had gone on long enough. She moved close to him, put her arms around his neck, and moved in to kiss him. It was a long, drawn-out, utterly satisfying kiss, but they both finally needed to come up for air.

67

"Let's go upstairs," Paul muttered. "Leaning against the door is not ideal."

The thought of going upstairs with Paul was more than tempting. "I don't know if that's such a good idea," Lee protested half-heartedly, as she pinned him against the door. "I mean, we've got to work together, you know."

"Right," said Paul, taking her hand and starting to lead her up the stairs. "What I had in mind was work—but in more comfortable quarters."

"Work? Is that what you consider it?" Lee tried to pull her hand out of his grasp but couldn't quite manage.

"Don't start an argument now, Masterson. Please?" He paused and kissed her, and she decided she had sufficiently protested and to just let him do the leading from now on. She only wished she had been more sober for their first encounter of an intimate nature.

Paul left the light on in the hall so that the bedroom was partially lit. He sat down on the side of the bed and stood her in front of him as he slowly removed her clothes. The buttons on her blouse gave him trouble until he just pulled it over her head instead. He sat and looked at her naked body for a moment.

"God, you're so beautiful."

Lee felt pleased that he thought so, but a little uncomfortable at being the only one undressed. She sat down next to him and helped him remove his clothes. When they were both naked, he laid back and held out his arms to her. They lay side by side, their arms and legs entwined, and once again he kissed her. She felt herself sinking down, down into a warm pool, and then abruptly the kiss ended. She waited expectantly for his next move. Nothing happened. She ran her fingers through his hair, her other hand feeling the contours of his back. Still he did nothing. Thinking perhaps he wanted her to be aggressive, she got a little more daring, her hand running up along the inside of his thigh. Still no response.

"Are you sure you're not gay?" she teased him, expecting to hear his familiar chuckle. Nothing. She lifted herself up and looked down at him. He had passed out, a beatific smile on his face.

Feeling a little bit relieved and a great deal of disappointment, she put a pillow under his head, covered him up, put her clothes back on, and went downstairs. She was suddenly totally sober. She went into the kitchen and made herself an early breakfast before going to bed on the couch. Her last thought before falling asleep was that she was henceforth going to swear off drinking.

CHAPTER SEVEN

When Lee next opened her eyes, sunlight was streaming in through the windows of the den. She glanced at the clock and saw that it was past ten. She wondered briefly why she was sleeping on the couch, then remembered with a rush. A warm feeling spread over her body as she thought of what had transpired only a few hours before. It was really rather funny in retrospect. Paul had finally gotten around to making a move, then had passed out before he could complete it. She wasn't sure he would see the humor in the situation, however.

Oh, well, it was only Saturday morning. They would have two whole days with nothing to do but get to know each other better. And if she had anything to say about it, they'd do it sans liquor. A couple of beers, maybe, but they could handle beer. It wasn't as though it would be a hardship; they both preferred eating to drinking.

She wondered if she was falling in love with him. She was certainly physically attracted to him. She also liked him, at least most of the time. Not when he treated her like a child, but he hadn't done much of that lately. She liked the way he looked, liked his quick mind, his sense of humor. Of course he was sarcastic some of the time, but then so was she. And they had a lot in common: the theater, baseball, food . . . well, there were probably lots of other things too. But none of the above would mean a thing unless they were also sexually compatible. She didn't see any reason why they shouldn't be, but you never knew.

Who knows, maybe he *always* passed out at the crucial moment. No, she felt sure that was the heavy drinking. Still, they wouldn't really know until they tried. But then, they'd have all weekend to try.

She wondered if he was awake yet. Maybe he was just lying in bed upstairs hoping she would join him. Just thinking about it made her very eager to find out.

She sat up on the couch, wishing she had a sexy black lace nightgown to wear. She settled for her beige lace bikinis, and headed for the stairs.

She went up noiselessly, hoping to surprise him. She paused in the doorway and looked at him asleep in the bed, sunlight fully on his face, the purple butterflies looking garish in the daylight. She walked over to the bed and looked down at him. He was on his back, sleeping soundly, the sheet twisted around one leg, his arms flung out to his sides. She stood there admiring his body: sturdy, well-muscled legs, narrow hips, flat stomach, a chest with just the right amount of hair in which to nestle one's face. Her eyes slid down again. Yes, he was well built in all the right places. She sighed audibly and reached out a hand to smooth his hair out of his eyes. He groaned at her touch and rolled over.

As long as he was still sleeping soundly, Lee decided to take a shower, shave her legs, and brush her teeth. She might as well be fresh when she went to him for the first time. She thought of washing her hair, but decided he might not find wet hair romantic in bed. Afterward she could wash her hair—when they showered together.

She made as much noise as possible while she was in the bathroom, hoping he'd wake up of his own accord. When she came out she had a large beach towel wrapped around her. She had seen a movie once where the girl was wrapped in a towel which she slowly unfolded to reveal herself to her lover. It had been a very erotic scene and Lee had never forgotten it. Not that Paul hadn't seen her body before he passed out, but the light hadn't been that good.

She went out and stood beside his bed, but he was still sleeping soundly. "Good morning, darling," she murmured in what she hoped was a low, sexy voice. But it was too low and he didn't hear her.

She reached out a hand and gently shook his shoulder. "Want me to join you?" She lowered her lids seductively and wet her lips. Nothing. She shook his shoulder a little harder.

"Hey, Paul, want to continue where we left off?" Either she was doing something wrong or he hadn't sobered up yet. Well, they had gotten in late; he'd barely had six hours' sleep. But how could he sleep at a time like this?

Maybe a loud noise was what was needed. She went over and slammed the bathroom door as hard as she could.

He leaped up in the bed, wild-eyed. "What the hell was that?" Then, groaning deeply, his hands went to his head. "Oh, my God, I'm dying!"

Lee walked into his line of vision. Or rather what would be his line of vision if he opened his eyes. Suddenly she felt nervous, unsure of what she was doing. She couldn't remember ever having been so aggressive before. "Good morning. How are you feeling?"

He slowly opened his bloodshot eyes and gave her a look of pure disbelief mixed with hatred. "Close the damned drapes."

She thought for a moment she had misinterpreted his look. It was obviously lust and he preferred making love in the dark. She quickly moved to the window and pulled the cord, shutting out most of the light.

"Now get the hell out of here and let me sleep!"

She stood for a moment in shocked disbelief that she was offering herself to him and he was rejecting her. It didn't take long for the shocked disbelief to turn to unadulterated anger.

"I'll get out of here all right," she informed him in a voice that was anything but seductive. "And I won't be

73

back either, do you understand me? Do you? Not if you beg me, not if you plead with me—not for *anything*, do you hear me? Do you?" She walked over to the bed and glared down at him. But she could have saved herself the trouble; he was once more sleeping soundly.

Making as much noise as she could, Lee went to the closet and got out her Nikes, running shorts, and T-shirt. She put them on quickly, reopened the drapes, and, as a final shot, slammed the bedroom door as she left.

She also slammed the front door and took off down the sidewalk at a fast run. It was hot and muggy and the sweat was pouring off her body, but after a few blocks she realized she was feeling a lot better. The anger was dissipating; she seemed to be working the effects of the vodka out of her system, and she was very close to starving to death. She slowed down and unzipped the pocket in her shorts, reaching inside. She usually kept a five-dollar bill there for just such emergencies. Yes, it was there. The next coffee shop she came to, she went inside.

She sat by herself in a booth, not wanting to offend the people at the counter with her less-than-sweet-smelling self.

The waiter came and took her order of melon, pancakes, eggs, sausages, and coffee, and Lee gulped down the glass of water he had brought her.

"Hello. You're Lee Masterson, aren't you?"

Lee recognized the sweet, dulcet tones even before she looked up to see Christie Sumner standing there. "Oh, hello. How are you doing, Christie?"

"Well, I'm just so thrilled about getting that part, I can't tell you. I talked to my agent on the phone last night and he said, 'Baby, this one's going to make you a star.' "

Lee remembered her manners. "Would you like to sit down?"

Christie slid into the other side of the booth.

"Where are you from, Christie?"

"Texas. You couldn't tell, could you?"

"No, not at all."

"Thank goodness, I had all these speech lessons to get rid of my accent. Where are you from, Miss Masterson?"

"Call me Lee." She was sure the ingenue across from her was every bit as old as she was and she didn't feel like being called Miss Masterson like she was one of her teachers. "I'm from California."

"Oh, that's where I want to go next. Everyone tells me I could be one of Charlie's Angels, but I think it's important to get known in New York first. They really respect New York actresses out on the Coast."

The waiter started loading the table with Lee's food. Christie asked him for a cup of coffee—black.

"I have to watch my weight," she explained to Lee in a serious tone. "Every little ounce shows up on the camera, you know."

Lee felt like asking what camera she was referring to, but stifled her impulse to be rude. She didn't really know what it was about Christie she didn't like. Maybe it was because the girl reminded her of a cheerleader. Lee never could tolerate cheerleaders. Or baton twirlers.

"Were you ever a cheerleader, Christie?"

With an effort, the girl drew her eyes away from Lee's breakfast. "Yes. In my senior year I was even head cheerleader and homecoming queen. It's on my résumé. I was also runner-up for Miss Texas."

"Very impressive," said Lee, managing to keep a straight face.

"Well, you and I know how important those things are, but Easterners don't go in so much for beauty contests and cheerleading. You were really lucky to grow up in California—the Rose Bowl parade and all that." Her eyes were again drawn to Lee's food.

Christie was beginning to make Lee feel decidedly greedy. "Would you care for some of my breakfast?"

"Oh, no, I couldn't possibly. Anyway, I only eat natural foods. I don't like to put poisons into my body."

Lee was enjoying every bit of the poison and even caught the waiter's eye, requesting a couple of jelly donuts just to top it off. "Yes, well, luckily I'm not an actress so I can indulge myself."

Christie looked her over carefully. "You have a really nice figure. You're lucky you don't have to worry about your weight. If I even look at something sweet I gain weight. How old are you, if you don't mind my asking. You look awfully young to be a playwright."

"I'm twenty-eight. How old are you?"

"My resume says twenty-two," Christie told her, looking down at the table. "But confidentially, I'm older than that. In this business, though, it's never too early to start lying about your age. Some actresses, with facelifts and all, play ingenues for years."

Lee was having second thoughts about whether it was worth having Christie play Dora in order to get Richard Jesse. She looked at her watch, trying to think of an excuse to get out of the girl's company. "I better be getting back. Paul will wake up and wonder where I am."

"Paul?"

"Yes. Paul Devon."

Christie's eyes widened. "You live with Paul Devon?"

"No, I wouldn't call it living with him. I'm just staying there. He has a big apartment and puts up the guest playwrights."

"But you're all alone with Paul Devon in his apartment?"

"Sure. But there's plenty of room."

"Oh, that man is *so* sexy, I could just *die!*"

Lee thought of taking Christie home with her and parading her upstairs to view Paul. Sexy indeed!

Lee asked for the bill. "Well, I guess I'll see you on Monday, Christie."

The girl looked disappointed that Lee was leaving. "Okay, Lee. And listen, I really want to thank you for giving me this chance."

Lee felt like telling Christie that "Sexy" was the one who gave her her chance, but she sensed this would undermine the actress's confidence. "I'll be looking forward to hearing you read on Monday," she told Christie before she left, chiding herself for not giving the girl a fair chance. If Christie hadn't been so pretty, and if Paul hadn't seemed so interested, she probably would have seen the girl's potential herself. Maybe.

It was afternoon when Lee got back to the apartment. It was quiet when she opened the front door and at first she thought Paul was still sleeping. But then she heard the sound of the shower in the downstairs bathroom. She went upstairs to take her own shower, feeling a distinct need for one after her long run, and when she was dressed again, this time in jeans and T-shirt, she went downstairs and found Paul in the kitchen.

He was looking far more cheerful than the last time she had seen him awake. "How about some breakfast?" he asked her.

"I've already eaten, but I'll have another cup of coffee with you." She saw his look of disappointment; he had probably hoped to finagle her into doing the cooking, she thought, then quickly revised her thinking when he started to put together an omelet with the ease of an experienced cook.

He caught her look. "You don't need to be impressed; omelets are the only thing I know how to cook. But they are first rate, if I do say so myself."

"No doubt you impress all your ladyfriends who stay for breakfast."

"No doubt." He grinned at her.

He seemed to be acting perfectly normal, as though nothing at all had occurred the night before. Of course nothing actually *had* happened, but it almost had, and Lee had hoped it would be out in the open so that they could discuss it. But far from discussing it, he wasn't even alluding to it, and she didn't know quite what to think.

"Did you have a good time at the party?" He was flipping over the omelet with an expert's ease.

"Yes. It was very interesting. And delicious food." He was making her feel decidedly ill at ease with his offhand manner. The water boiled, and she made two cups of instant coffee and carried them over to the table.

"Did you get to meet Truman Capote?"

"Truman Capote wasn't there."

"Sure he was—over by the piano singing along." He slid the omelet out of the pan and onto a plate.

"Well, I didn't see him. I met Lauren Bacall in the bathroom, though, combing her hair." If he wanted to joke around, she could do it too.

"I'm embarrassed to ask you this," he said, sitting down with her, "but how did I end up in the bedroom? You're the guest; I don't want you to make a habit of sleeping on the couch."

She tried to keep her expression neutral as she took in the fact that he didn't remember what had happened the night before. She should have realized that if he had had enough to drink to pass out that quickly, there was also a possibility of his not remembering what had transpired, but it just hadn't occurred to her.

"You know," he was saying, "I had this crazy dream about you. Only natural, I suppose, your staying here and all, but I generally don't have such vivid dreams. And in color."

She could only look at him and hope he wasn't going to say what she thought he was going to say.

He said it. "I had this dream that you came into the bedroom while I was sleeping and . . . well, anyway, it was really vivid. Enjoyable too."

Lee could feel the flush mounting slowly from her neck on up, and only hoped it wouldn't be noticeable under her tan. Wrong again.

"You don't need to blush—it was only a dream. And it was obviously in my mind, not yours."

Lee was wishing a hole would open up in the kitchen floor so that she could just disappear from his sight. Thank goodness he thought it was a dream, at least. If he didn't remember the night before, it would be a little difficult to explain her presence in his bedroom in the morning.

"You know what we're going to do today?" He was certainly sounding cheerful, not at all like someone who was having a giant hangover should sound.

"You're taking me to Central Park?"

"No, we're going down to the theater so that you can do your revisions. I've got to meet with some of the technical people."

"On a Saturday?"

"We start rehearsing Monday. Might as well get the revisions typed up so that we can get them run off and have the revised script in the actors' hands on Monday."

"You're the boss."

"That's what I like to hear—proper respect for the director."

Lee looked around the kitchen at the mess he had made. "Proper respect doesn't include cleaning up after you."

He laughed. "I was afraid of that."

CHAPTER EIGHT

At six o'clock he stuck his head in the door of the small room he had left her in to do her revisions. "All finished?"

"Almost. Do you want to read them?"

He took the papers from her and sat down to read them while she finished up the last pages.

"This is great—just great," he said when he had finished looking over the changes. "And extending the ideas over into the second act was just what it needed. I think we have a play, Masterson."

Lee was pleased by his enthusiasm. "I hadn't realized that was what the second act needed. It really does make more sense this way."

"Absolutely!"

"That's it, then? No more revisions?"

He laughed. "No more till we start rehearsing. One thing you've got to learn, Lee, is that a playwright's work isn't done until opening night. Sometimes not even then. But you've got the basics. The only changes now will probably just be bits of dialogue that'll get changed when we hear it done."

Lee was willing to sit there and listen to him tell her how good her play was for the rest of the night, but he got up and reached out a hand to her.

"Come on, you've done a good day's work. I'm going to take you out on the town to celebrate."

Lee hesitated. "I don't know whether I feel like drinking so much again."

"Can't handle your liquor, huh?"

She gave him what she hoped was a withering look. "*I* can handle it, I was worried about you."

"You talking about last night? I wasn't so bad last night, was I? It was just that I was tired, and then all that drinking on an empty stomach."

"I don't think you *ever* have an empty stomach," Lee told him.

He laughed. "Not if I can help it. I'm rather like a certain female playwright I know in that respect."

They gave Frank the revised script to be run off before leaving the theater, then went home and changed their clothes before going out. Paul told her he was going to take her to a fancy place, so Lee put on the one dress she had brought along in anticipation of opening night—a clinging, lightweight knit in a soft shade of brown that was flattering to both her figure and her suntan.

He gave a low whistle when she walked down the stairs, his eyes taking in her braless contours. "I don't know if it's safe walking down the street with you in that dress."

"We can stay away from subways and Central Park," Lee remarked, feeling uneasy under his gaze. The dress was perfectly proper; she had worn it to school functions. She supposed it was because he was used to seeing her in such casual clothes. He was looking awfully good himself. Dark blue pants, slim and well-fitting, a silky-looking shirt in beige. Even a lightweight sport coat over his arm. And he smelled of something delicious; some men's fragrance she had never smelled before.

She paused on the bottom step, on eye level with him. "It's nice to see you in something besides a Mickey Mouse T-shirt. If I had known you liked him so much, I would have brought you one from Disneyland."

His eyes glittered. "I get the feeling you have trouble saying nice things to me."

She raised an eyebrow. "You look gorgeous, Mr. Devon. And that smell is delicious."

"Come closer and you can smell it better," he said in a low voice, his eyes mocking her. He put his hands on her shoulders, then slowly moved them down her arms, making her skin tingle at his touch. "You, Ms. Masterson, look good enough to eat. Perhaps we should forgo dinner and just stay home. I'm sure we could amuse ourselves."

Lee gave him a wicked smile. "I'm sure we could. If I'm not mistaken, the Yankee game is being televised tonight."

He put his arms around her back and drew her against him, his face not two inches from hers. "Ah, what a romantic you are, Ms. Masterson."

"Rather like you, Mr. Devon?"

His hands were moving up and down her back, making breathing difficult.

"Maybe we should stay home. We could open up the couch in the den, have a few drinks, watch the ballgame together . . ."

At the mention of a few drinks, memories of the night before came flooding back to Lee. Yes, she mused, a few drinks, then you'll pass out on the couch and that will be the end of another unforgettable night. She pulled away from him and headed for the front door.

"I know I said something wrong," he said, "but for the life of me I can't figure out what."

"I was just suddenly overcome with hunger," Lee said. "I didn't have any lunch today."

"I want you to know," he told her when they settled back in the taxi, "I'm going there only for you."

"Isn't Tavern-on-the-Green in Central Park?"

"Yes, but not too far in. And we'll take a taxi out of there too."

They ate in the Crystal Room, a specially glassed-in portion of the restaurant that looked out over the park. Wine was served with the dinner, but Lee didn't drink much and noticed that Paul didn't either. She had just enough to give her a glow, but she wasn't certain whether the warm feeling she was experiencing was from the wine or the nearness of Paul.

He was attentive throughout the meal, asking her about her life in California, questioning her about teaching, inquiring whether she would consider moving to New York.

"I don't think there's anyplace like it. Of course I've never lived anywhere else," he admitted.

"You went to school here too?"

"Studied directing at NYU—right in the Village."

"More than anything else, I want to keep on writing plays," Lee told him. "And New York's the place to be for that. It's also got an element of danger I like. California's so nice and safe and dull."

"What do you mean, an element of danger?"

"The way you're afraid to take subways or walk in the park. I kind of like that; I always longed to live dangerously—be a spy or something."

"Are you crazy?" He sounded upset. "I don't want to hear about you doing anything silly, you hear me?"

"I'm not a child, Paul."

"Well, you sound like one. What are you going to do when I'm not around to protect you?"

Lee was surprised he was getting so serious. "I can take care of myself—I've been doing it for twenty-eight years."

He lighted a cigarette and she could see his hand shake. "Yeah, out in sunny California. Listen to me, Masterson — being careful in New York is nothing to joke about."

"If I thought I'd end up as paranoid as you, I wouldn't stay here."

"Paranoid? You think I'm paranoid? Do you see burglar alarms or windowgates around my apartment? I'm not paranoid; I just use my head. And you'd better too!"

She was sorry she had said anything. They had been getting along so well and now he was angry with her. "Hey, Paul, I'm sorry. I was just teasing you. I'm the most careful person alive, honest. You should see me drive the freeways—fifty-five miles per hour, staying in the right-hand lane." This wasn't exactly an accurate description of the way she drove, but anything to calm him down. "I even took a course in self-defense at the Women's Center. Want a demonstration?"

"I think I'll forgo the demonstration," Paul said, a slow smile softening his face. "Sorry I came down so hard; I would just hate to see anything happen to you." He reached over and took her hand, its warmth seeming to spread over her body. "Want to go dancing someplace?"

Lee shook her head. "I'm a terrible dancer."

Paul breathed a sigh of relief. "Thank God! I haven't danced since high school, and then only when I was forced to. What would you like to do? Just name it."

Lee smiled. "You mean that?"

"Sure, it's your night, Merilee Masterson."

Lee's eyes gleamed. "All right then; what I'd really like to do is ride in one of those carriages around the park. You know, the ones with the horses."

He looked at her in disbelief. "You've got to be kidding!"

"Not at all."

"Those are for tourists!"

"Well, I'm a tourist."

Paul poured himself some more wine. "What if someone recognized me?"

"Oh, come on, Paul."

"I'm serious. What if someone I know should see me. I'd never live it down."

Lee poured herself some more wine, prepared to do battle. "So you tell them you were humoring a visiting playwright. I think it would be lovely, like something from another century. A horse-drawn carriage beneath the stars . . ."

"Oh, no, a romantic!" He gulped down his wine.

"What's the matter with being a romantic?"

"I thought you were different."

"Ninety percent of the time I'm a pragmatist. Ten percent of the time I'm a romantic. This evening just happens to fall in the ten-percent category."

"I lucked out, huh?"

"Sarcasm will get you nowhere."

If Paul was reluctant when they first started out, he soon thawed out and actually seemed to be enjoying himself. It was a clear night, the moon and stars were all out, and the view from the park of the tall buildings surrounding it was spectacular.

They had been riding for about ten minutes when Paul put his arm around Lee. "Enjoying yourself, Masterson?"

"It's lovely."

"As romantic as you pictured?"

She turned to him. "Almost."

"What's lacking?"

"The prince." She felt his arm stiffen.

"Prince?"

"To be perfectly romantic, I'd be in the carriage with a prince."

Paul considered this for a moment in silence. "To a playwright, a director *is* a prince." Before she could think of a proper retort, he had drawn her to him and closed his mouth over hers, effectively cutting off her speech.

Far from minding, Lee gave herself up to the kiss, happy he was at last acting the way a prince should act. He turned in the seat, pulling her closer to him, his tongue tracing the outline of her mouth, one hand caressing her back, the other smoothing her hair away from her face.

She reached up her hands and pulled his head closer, leaning back against the side of the carriage. He stopped kissing her for a moment and she opened her eyes.

"This is a bit public, isn't it?" he asked in a husky voice.

She glanced around. They were in a deserted section of the park. "Don't worry, Paul, I'll protect you. I know karate," she teased him.

He gave a low chuckle. "You better start protecting

yourself, my dear." He was over her body before he finished speaking, his lips hard upon her mouth, his tongue gaining entry. She felt his hand slide down from her hair, pass softly over her neck and make its way slowly down, stopping when it reached one taut breast thrust toward him. She moaned as his fingers found her nipple, erect and sensitive, and she pushed herself against his hand, wishing the material between his fingers and her flesh would disappear.

He stopped and she opened her eyes, half dazed, filled with a desire she had forgotten existed.

"What's the matter?" she murmured.

He sat back and lighted a cigarette. "This is like high school—making out in the back seat of a car. Let's go home. I want to make love to you properly. I want to be able to see your body, have you see mine."

She sat up next to him and took his hand. "Yes, let's go home."

By the time they entered the apartment, Lee was dizzy with wanting him. It had been a long time since she had felt like this about any man, and she sensed that Paul was as overwhelmed by his emotions as she was. As soon as he locked the door behind them, he took her in his arms, and once again she felt herself drowning in ecstasy as he kissed her deeply, his tongue thrusting into her mouth. He let out a moan as her teeth closed gently over it.

He stopped, looking down at her with dark eyes filled with warmth, then took her hand and led her toward the stairs.

"Shall we give it another try?" he quipped.

She stopped short. "*What?*"

"I think we'll be more successful than last night," he chuckled.

"You *did* remember!" Lee accused him.

"Did you really think I could forget something like that?"

"And you let me think—"

"I thought it would be less embarrassing for you that way."

She raised an eyebrow. "Well, let's get started before you pass out again."

He laughed in enjoyment. "God, you're refreshing. You're the only woman I know who retains a sense of humor—"

"In bed?"

"That remains to be seen," he laughed with pleasure. "Come along, wench—the night is young. . . ."

"I can really live without clichés in bed," murmured Lee, causing Paul to laugh so hard he had to sit down on the stairs to recover.

"I said I appreciated a sense of humor," he said when he could talk again. "I didn't ask for a stand-up comic."

"Actually, except for *Alekos,* I've mostly written comedy," Lee said seriously.

"Masterson," he growled at her, "are we going to make love or are we going to engage in a discussion of your writing techniques?"

"I'd enjoy either one," said Lee, trying not to laugh.

"I guarantee you'll enjoy this more," promised Paul, getting up and continuing up the stairs, holding her hand tightly.

He switched on the overhead light in the bedroom and Lee glanced at the tangled mess he had made of the bed. She thought of straightening it, then reconsidered. It would be a worse mess than that when they were done making love; she could put it to rights afterward.

Paul stood facing her, watching her eyes as he slowly unbuttoned his shirt. He removed it, dropping it on the floor, and his hands reached next for his belt. He undid it quickly, then unzipped his pants and let them fall around his ankles. He sat down on the bed to remove his shoes and socks, still watching her.

Lee stood as though mesmerized, following his every move. When at last he stood, naked, clearly as excited as

88

she was, she found herself trembling with desire. He came over to her and with a swift motion, lifted her dress up over her head and dropped it on the floor with his clothes. She stood there, clothed only in brief bikini panties, her breasts glowing white against the tan of her skin. His eyes raked her body and she felt her nipples growing taut, and a swift warmth swept through her.

She kicked off her shoes, then slid her panties down. They moved together, their bodies warm and slightly damp. The hair on his chest rubbed against her nipples and she cried out, lifting her mouth to his.

His kiss was rough and demanding; his hands roamed freely over her body causing her to lose that last semblance of control that still remained. She pressed closer to him, closer still, wanting their bodies to join, to be one.

His hand moved between her legs, probing, exploring, and such waves of excitement flowed through her body that she would have collapsed if he hadn't been holding her. He backed her toward the bed and gently eased her down on it, his body following, covering hers with its weight and its warmth.

"Lee, my lovely Lee," he murmured in sensuous tones, taking his time, his expert hands raising her emotions to a fevered pitch.

"Oh, Paul," she gasped, "don't stop—please don't stop."

"My sweet darling," he whispered, his mouth brushing over her ear, "is this what you want? Is it?"

"Yes, yes," she gasped, arching her body up against his, her hands exploring him with a will of their own.

The phone rang, shattering the moment. They tried to ignore it.

It continued ringing, an insistent intrusion, until Paul, swearing in anger, rolled off Lee and reached down to pick it up where it lay on the floor beside the bed.

"Hello?" His voice was curt, unwelcoming.

Lee hoped he would get rid of whoever it was quickly.

She rolled toward him, one hand caressing his body as he listened to the caller.

"Oh, God, no—how terrible for you."

She felt his body tense from what he was hearing and removed her hand from his thigh.

"Yes, yes, of course. . . . I'll be right over, soon as I can throw on some clothes and get a taxi. Take it easy, okay? I'll be there soon."

He hung up the phone, turned to Lee, and heaved a big sigh. "My girl, I do believe someone up there is determined to keep us apart. That was my mother."

Lee was still too aroused to think clearly. "Your mother is trying to keep us apart?"

"No, my mother's not up there, my mother's over in Brooklyn. Her apartment was broken into tonight when she was out."

"Oh, Paul, how awful!"

He stood up and started to get dressed. "She lives alone; my father died two years ago. The police have been there but she's upset, frightened. She wants me to come over."

"Of course. You must." Lee pulled the sheet up over her. "Is it a long trip?"

"No, just across the river in Brooklyn Heights. About ten minutes from here." He went into the bathroom and she could hear him splashing water on his face.

When he came back, he leaned over the bed and kissed her. "Better get some sleep. I don't know when I'll be back." He started to chuckle.

"What's so funny?"

He shook his head in disbelief. "The second aborted attempt in two nights. You think we ought to forget the whole thing?"

"No, I don't think so," Lee drawled.

His eyes gleamed. "Neither do I. And you know something, Masterson? I think you're going to be worth waiting for."

He turned off the overhead light as he left, and Lee,

feeling too weak to get up and straighten the bed, remained as she was.

She couldn't get to sleep and asked herself if she was falling in love with Paul. The answer was a resounding yes. She certainly hadn't anticipated falling in love in New York, but neither was she averse to the idea. She had lived alone since she was twenty-one, all her adult years. It would be nice to have the companionship of a man she loved, and the fact that both their interests lay in the theater was an added bonus. A playwright and a director —what a perfect combination, she mused. Of course she'd have to do something about getting him to clear some of his "memorabilia" out of the living room—make it more habitable. And the purple butterflies would have to go. All in all, they suited each other admirably. Lee no longer had any qualms about whether they'd be sexually compatible; there seemed little doubt that that was going to be every bit as exciting as the lovemaking before the phone call had been.

Her last thoughts before falling asleep were of a wedding taking place on the stage of the Village Playhouse.

CHAPTER NINE

"I won't be home until this evening. Can you amuse yourself without me?"

It was noon and the phone had awakened her. "How's your mother?"

"Pretty good. I'm going to install another lock on her door while I'm here. The one she's got can be opened with a credit card."

Lee wondered if New York burglars carried credit cards. "I can amuse myself. I think I'll take a subway ride up to the park."

"Listen, do I have to worry about my mother *and* you? There's an art show over in Washington Square Park. You could walk over there, have a look . . ."

"I don't like art shows."

"Don't they have any culture in southern California?"

"Every shopping mall in California has an art show," Lee informed him. "I'd rather watch a baseball game."

"So would I," he admitted. "Anyway, I'll see you tonight." He paused. "Miss me?"

"No."

"*No?*"

"I just woke up. I'll miss you later."

"See that you do," he muttered before saying good-bye.

Lee got dressed in running shoes, shorts, and a tank top, and left the apartment. She wasn't interested in the art show, but did want to see Washington Square Park.

It was a beautiful day, the humidity not nearly as high

as it had been previously. And the sky was so blue, unlike California skies, which are usually rather greenish from the overlay of smog. There were lots of other joggers out and she asked directions from one and found that the park was only a few blocks from Paul's apartment.

Ringed by the art show, which seemed to be attracting a lot of tourists, the park was filled with people, most of them appearing to be college students. There were lots of weekend athletes, some running, some playing baseball, some throwing Frisbees around. There were people playing chess, some guitar players, a jazz group, people walking dogs and babies, and, in the center of the park, a group of roller skaters dancing to disco music. This made Lee feel immediately at home; the roller-skating craze had started in southern California, after all.

She was watching the skaters and not where she was walking when she tripped over a dog leash and went sprawling down on the path. Someone helped her up and she heard a concerned voice ask, "Are you all right?"

Aside from being covered with dirt and feeling foolish, she was quite unharmed. She looked up into the face of the man she had talked to at the party. "Oh, hello," she said.

He gave her a quizzical look. "Do I know you? You look familiar but I can't seem to place . . ."

"Gene," she said, "Gene Lesnek, isn't it? We met at Harry Duke's party."

"Of course," he said, "the playwright. Although you look ten years younger in the daylight."

"I'm afraid it's the clothes, and the dirt, and maybe the pigtails," she explained, wishing she hadn't run into someone she knew. But then she wouldn't be so dirty if she hadn't fallen over the dog leash. The dog itself, a fluffy little black-and-white mutt, was jumping up on her legs. She reached down to pet him.

"Perfect attire for a Sunday in the park," he said graciously, although he was dressed impeccably in a cream-colored suit. "Down, Malvolio," he ordered the dog, but the dog ignored him. "I was trying to impress you," he laughed, "hoping for once he'd obey me."

"Do you live around here?" asked Lee.

"Right over there." He pointed to one of the town-houses on the north side of the park. "Lovely view of the park, but the noise can get pretty bad sometimes. Particularly if the students are out here protesting something." He seemed to consider for a moment, then asked her, "Would you like to come see my place? Perhaps have a glass of lemonade?"

"I think I'm too dirty to be invited into your house," said Lee.

"Not at all, but in any case I had the terrace in mind. It's lovely and quite shady this time of day."

"Thank you. Then I'd love a glass of lemonade."

He led her through a living room decorated exactly to her taste—a large fireplace with a lovely painting over the mantel, two walls lined with bookshelves and filled with books, big comfortable chairs to read in, and lots of light from French doors leading out to the terrace. She looked around with pleasure. "What a charming room. Have you ever been to Paul's place?"

Gene looked as if he was trying not to laugh. "Yes. Quite interesting."

"He calls it memorabilia," Lee said with a straight face.

"Memorabilia? I see."

"In California we call people like him packrats."

Gene couldn't contain his laughter. "Yes, we call them that here also. But I don't want to cast aspersions on Paul's taste; after all, he did find you."

"Very nice of you to say, but he didn't find me at all; he found my play."

"I'm sure your play is lovely also."

"You'll have to come see it and see for yourself," she told him.

"I plan to," he said. "Now go out on the terrace and

make yourself comfortable while I get the lemonade. Or would you prefer something stronger?"

"Lemonade would be perfect." She walked out onto his brick terrace and sat down on one of the chaise longues. It was quiet and peaceful, two large trees providing plenty of shade. It was hard for her to believe that she was in the middle of a big city. She wondered if Paul had a terrace. No, of course he didn't—how could he possibly have a terrace when his apartment was the top two floors. She really must stop thinking like a Californian. But being able to sit outdoors was something she would miss in New York. That is, if she decided to stay in the city. She might be jumping to conclusions, Paul might not even want her to stay. But she thought he did. She hoped he did.

Gene came out with a tray holding a pitcher of lemonade, two glasses, and a plate of cookies and Lee remembered she hadn't eaten at all that day. She helped herself to both. Malvolio put his paws up on her lap and she gave him a bite of her cookie.

"Are you enjoying New York?" he asked her.

"Very much, it's all been quite exciting so far. Of course from now on we'll get into rehearsing the play and I won't be seeing much of the city, I don't suppose, but, for me at least, that will probably be even more exciting. I don't know if you can understand this, but coming to New York and having my play produced is having a fantasy I've had for years come true. Sometimes I think I will suddenly wake up and it will all have been a dream."

"Well, in a way I understand," he told her. "I rather felt the same way about coming to New York. "I'm from Romania, you see, and when I was younger, New York, in fact the entire United States, was a fantasy of mine; I always dreamed of coming here. And then later it became a necessity. I found it very difficult to function in a place where freedom has so many restrictions."

Lee told him that was the theme of her play, the inability of some people to function without freedom. He told her about life in Romania, the good parts and the bad, about the relatives he left behind, and about his successful escape. She found him fascinating and most congenial to talk to, but there wasn't the spark between them that there was between her and Paul. Which was a perversity of hers, of course, as she and Gene got on much better than she probably ever would with Paul. She liked a little excitement to life, though, and for the moment Paul seemed to be providing a full measure of that.

She left for home around four, stopping at a grocery store along the way so that she could fix an easy dinner for herself and Paul. She didn't think he would want to go out to eat and she would be quite content to stay at home. She hoped he wouldn't think she was becoming quite domesticated; she knew herself it was only a novelty to her, one that would soon pass. Cooking and cleaning house and all the rest would never give her the kind of satisfaction that writing a play did.

She put away the groceries, took a shower and washed her hair, and was downstairs looking for something to read when she heard a key in the lock. She ran to the door.

"Hey, sweetheart, miss me?" He looked exhausted but managed a tired smile for her.

Lee nodded.

"Did you go out and eat?"

"I bought some steaks and stuff. I thought we'd eat in." She followed him into the den where he promptly collapsed on the couch.

"I'm beat—never did get any sleep at my mother's."

"Is she okay?"

"Yeah, she's fine. A tough old bird; you'll have to meet her sometime. Only thing the burglar took was some silverware and a portable TV that doesn't work. And her insurance will cover both. What time's dinner?"

"I can start it now," Lee said. "It'll take an hour for the potatoes to bake."

"Do you mind if I grab an hour's sleep? I'll be good as new after a nap."

"Sure. I'll wake you when it's ready."

"Give me a little kiss before you go," he said to her, and she leaned down to him. He was too tired to put much effort into it and was asleep before she left the room.

She tried to wake him when dinner was ready, but he only rolled away from her, muttering in his sleep. Lee decided he needed rest more than food; anyway, his mother had undoubtedly fed him.

She sat down in the kitchen and ate her dinner. When she was finished, she decided to eat his as well since it wouldn't keep.

After doing the dishes, she went upstairs to work on her play. At eleven she went back down, hoping Paul would be awake and they could talk for a while, but he was still sleeping soundly, so she turned the air-conditioner to low, covered him with an afghan, and went to bed.

CHAPTER TEN

"Okay, we're going to have a read-through just to get a sense of the story. Don't try getting into your parts yet," Paul had advised the actors, but by scene two they were reading with a great deal of dramatic intent despite his advice to the contrary.

It was the first time Lee had heard the play read aloud, and the characters were coming alive for her. So far it was just the men reading. Dora wouldn't appear until the middle of scene two, Athena in scene three.

When Christie started to read the part of Dora, Lee had all she could do not to noticeably wince. The girl was using a cooing sort of voice, the kind that could lapse into baby talk with just a little effort. Lee looked over at Paul to see how he was taking it. He appeared unconcerned. She glanced at the rest of the actors, but they all had their eyes on their scripts. Christie got to a line about the attempted assassination on the Colonels, but said *colonials* instead.

"Colonels," Lee corrected her.

Christie stopped reading. "I beg your pardon?"

"Colonels, not colonials. The Colonels are the dictators, the military junta that took over; colonials are inhabitants of colonies." Lee was congratulating herself on working in the word *junta* too, as the girl had twice pronounced the *j*.

The actress looked totally bewildered and clearly saw no distinction between Colonels and colonials.

"Let's get on with it," said Paul, sounding annoyed, and the reading continued.

The part of Dora that Christie was reading was that of a young militant intellectual, a graduate of law school, and as such had an extensive vocabulary. She made a couple of speeches to the Resistance group during the course of the scene, both speeches studded with many words over two syllables. Christie invariably mispronounced the difficult words and Lee began to correct her, keeping after the actress until she got the pronunciation right.

Paul, with sharp looks at Lee, allowed it to go on for a while before finally slamming his fist on the table, causing a couple of the actors to jump in alarm.

"Ms. Masterson, we are here for a *cold* reading. The actors are not yet familiar with their parts; that will come with time. Not only are you not contributing to the reading by your constant interruptions, you are getting very close to turning it into a shambles. What I suggest is we all take a fifteen-minute break and when we return we'll begin the reading again. At the beginning."

Lee sat in stunned silence as the actors filed out of the room.

Paul slowly lighted a cigarette before glancing over at Lee. "Well? Are you going to apologize?"

"You made a fool of me," said Lee between clenched teeth.

"You made a fool of yourself. That was the most unprofessional conduct I have ever witnessed at a reading in my entire career."

"That girl can't pronounce the simplest words. She's going to ruin my play."

"Actors aren't required to read. They're only required to act. She'll get the pronunciations right with time."

"You wouldn't say that if she wasn't so pretty," Lee blurted out, close to tears.

"Get hold of yourself, Masterson," Paul advised her curtly as he got up and went to the door. "You're behaving like a child. I expect occasional childish behavior from actors; I will not tolerate it in playwrights."

Lee was left alone in the room. When she felt she had the tears under control, she went out to get herself a cup of coffee, not wanting the actors to think she was sitting alone in disgrace, sulking.

Christie and Paul were standing together outside the door. Paul had his arm around the girl's shoulder, speaking to her softly. The rest of the group were standing around the table that held a coffeepot at the end of the hall.

Lee walked up to them, helping herself to some coffee. "I guess I should apologize to you," she told them. "I didn't know I wasn't supposed to speak during a reading."

Dan Roentch gave her an impish grin. "With Christie you have to teach her to pronounce long words phonetically—like learning a foreign language. Don't worry, she'll memorize the pronunciation all right. She'll never know the meaning of what she's saying, but it'll sound intelligible."

Lee was horrified, wondering how someone could give a believable performance if they didn't understand the subject matter. "Are you serious?"

Dan crossed his heart. "Absolutely. I've worked with her before."

"How does she ever get parts?" Lee asked him.

"Are you kidding?" asked Nonie. "If I had her looks, I'd be a star by now."

"Yeah, it's tough, Nonie," Dan said, winking at Lee. "With her looks and your talent you'd really go far."

"Thanks a lot, Dan," said Nonie, and the whole group laughed. While the girl didn't have the starlet kind of looks Christie possessed, Lee found her far more appealing.

"I don't think you should worry about Christie, Ms. Masterson," said Richard Jesse, his dark eyes intent on Lee.

"Oh, not Ms. Masterson—Lee, please, all of you," Lee told them.

Richard gave her a slow smile and Lee thought again what an incredibly handsome young man he was.

"Paul Devon is a fine director," Richard went on. "If he sees potential in Christie, I'm sure it's there. Anyway, directors can work miracles with actors."

"Luckily for us," quipped Dan, and Lee decided he was going to be the clown of the group. And the way things were going, they were going to need some comic relief.

"Yeah, but the potential he saw in her might not have anything to do with acting," Nonie pointed out, an ominous look on her expressive face.

"Paul's a professional," argued Richard. "He's just interested in the play."

"He's also a man," said Nonie, "and speaking of the man, he's trying to get our attention. I think the break is over, kids."

Richard took Lee aside before they went back in. "Seriously, Lee, there are a lot of actors who give lousy cold readings. It doesn't mean a thing."

They started the reading again. Most of the actors were better the second time. Christie was just as bad. Not only did she stumble over most of the words, but her wide-eyed look and little-girl voice were so opposed to the way Lee had conceived the character of Dora that Lee was almost sorry for having made the deal in order to get Richard. Not totally sorry, though—Richard was so perfect as Alekos she felt she could have written the play with him in mind. She thought that if Christie didn't improve drastically over the course of the rehearsals, she'd rewrite much of Dora's part, making it smaller and, perhaps, enlarging Dan's part. She wondered if she'd need Paul's permission to do that, but decided she didn't.

At least Christie wasn't in act two. Most of the second act consisted of Alekos's court martial where very few of the Resistance members from act one appeared. Well, if the audience doesn't leave after act one because of Christie, Lee thought, at least they'll be spared her presence in act two.

At noon Paul told the actors to take an hour for lunch. "You go with them, Lee, I'm going to stay here and work on the blocking."

"Do you want me to help you?" Lee asked him, hoping they could get back to the closeness they were enjoying before he had yelled at her so unreasonably.

"That's the director's province," he informed her tersely.

They went to a nearby coffee shop where everyone but Christie ordered hamburgers. She ordered two sandwiches to go, and when someone asked where she was going, she looked flustered and said that Paul had to eat and she was going to take him back a sandwich. The girl looked so vitally concerned that Lee could have kicked her.

"He's not going to thank you for bothering him," said Dan.

"I won't bother him," Christie protested. "I'll just sit quietly and study my lines."

Since no one could argue the fact that her lines needed studying, nothing more was said about it until Christie left.

"That girl's wasting her time," was Nonie's observation.

"You mean with Paul?" asked Richard.

Nonie nodded. "Oh, I'm not saying he wouldn't go to bed with her—I hear he's pretty human in that respect. But Christie's looking for more than that, and there's no way Paul Devon is going to get involved with an actress. With anyone even connected with the theater, for that matter."

Needless to say this came as something of a shock to Lee. "Why not? I would think it would be only natural for him to be involved with someone who shared his interests."

"Not after being burned once," said Nonie with an air of finality.

"What are you talking about?" asked Lee.

"I'm talking about his ex-wife—Jackie Flannery."

"The actress?"

"None other. She left Paul and ran off with a playwright. Although it's movie scripts he's writing now, I hear."

"From what I hear, Paul is still in love with her," said Dan.

"Well, they hadn't been married for long, and the guy *was* his best friend. That could be pretty traumatic," said Nonie. "You'll have to get used to it, Lee—the theater is the greatest place in the world for gossip."

Lee found she had lost her appetite by the time the hamburgers arrived. The knowledge that Paul had been married was news to her, of course, but by itself that fact wouldn't have bothered her. But if Paul was still in love with the woman, then that meant he had only been using her. Well, to be exact, attempting to use her. Probably because she was convenient. After all, staying in his apartment, what could be easier for the man? Her first reaction had been a deep unhappiness, but that soon turned to anger. She was thankful his two prior attempts at using her had been unsuccessful; she was darned sure he wasn't going to be given the opportunity a third time. How stupid of her to fall in love with the man before knowing anything about him. But then she had fallen in love with an unsuitable man once before and managed to get over it, rather quickly, too, as she recalled. But she very much wished she wasn't staying in his apartment.

"A penny for your thoughts," said Richard from the seat beside her. "And if you're not going to eat your hamburger . . ."

Lee found that she had regained her appetite and took a bite of the burger. "I was just thinking about Paul. I didn't know he had been married."

Nonie gave her a look of concern. "Me and my big mouth! You're not interested in him, are you?"

Lee smiled weakly. "We don't really get along very well."

Dan let out a roar of laughter. "That's an understatement if I ever heard one."

"I guess he had reason to be angry with me this morning," Lee said. "I've never had a play produced before. I don't know how I'm supposed to act."

"That's easy, we'll teach you," offered Dan. "First of all, the playwright should never interrupt the director."

"And treat him with the utmost respect at all times," Nonie chimed in.

"He is God and you are merely a mortal," instructed Richard.

"When he says, 'This scene doesn't seem to be working,' you rewrite," said Dan.

"Even if you have to stay up all night to do it," said Nonie.

"But the most important thing to remember," said Richard, "is the actors are merely pawns in the director's game."

"Not really human at all," added Dan.

"And not such as you would wish to socialize with," said Nonie. "I'm surprised he's allowing you to eat lunch with us. You're among the enemy camp, so to speak."

"*Allowing* me? I'll eat lunch with whomever I wish," Lee said defiantly. "I happen to find all of you terrific company. Anyway, I don't think he has much respect for women playwrights."

"He should now. It's a damn fine play," said Richard, and the others all murmured their agreement.

By the time they got back to the theater, Lee had half convinced herself she wasn't in love with Paul at all, that at most it was just a physical attraction. But one look at him upon her return disabused herself of that notion at once. She gave him a look full of regret and saw his

105

puzzled response, but they were surrounded by actors and he didn't say anything to her.

The afternoon's rehearsal took place in the theater where Paul had them walk through their parts on the stage while he gave them blocking to note in their scripts. Lee noticed that he completely ignored the blocking she had written into the script, and also saw that he was right in doing so. She watched him carefully, trying to determine why he had actors move when he did, wondering if she could ever try her own hand at directing. She knew the theory that playwrights weren't supposed to direct their own plays any more than lawyers were supposed to serve as their own counsel, but some had done it successfully nonetheless and she was certain that every playwright probably had the thought that she sometimes entertained, that they could direct their own work much better than anyone else.

At one point in the rehearsals the young blond whom Lee had seen Paul talking to at the party, came down the aisle and took the seat next to hers.

"I'm Carter Boone," he said to her, holding out his hand. "I'm designing the sets for your show and I have a few sketches I wanted to go over with Paul. Would you like to take a look?"

Lee nodded, and the young man passed her one sketch at a time, waiting for her reaction. They were wonderful, much better than she had envisioned them, and she told him so.

"Thanks. I only hope Paul agrees with you. He's a real perfectionist when it comes to sets. When it comes to anything having to do with one of the plays he directs, for that matter."

"I hadn't thought an off-Broadway theater would go to such expense," Lee admitted to him, impressed by the two elaborate sets he had designed.

"The Playhouse is in good shape financially, unlike some of the others," he told her, then stopped talking when Paul shouted down from the stage that he wanted silence.

Paul kept the actors until after nine that night, then dismissed them, calling for an early rehearsal the following day at eight A.M. Lee remained in her seat for a moment, waiting for him to join her, but, almost as an afterthought, he called down to her that she could leave too.

"I'll be here late working with the set designer," he told her. "You might as well go out and eat. Keep the check stub from the restaurant and we'll reimburse you."

Lee found Richard and Dan and Nonie standing out in front of the theater arguing about where to go to eat. When they found she was free for the rest of the evening, they asked her to join them, and she gladly accepted, not wanting to return to the empty apartment alone where she knew she would spend the evening wondering what to do about her conflicting feelings for Paul.

They took her to Downey's, a restaurant in the theater district that was a hangout for young actors, and they all ordered barbecued ribs and french fries and shared a couple of pitchers of beer. The talk revolved around the play for the most part, as it was quite naturally the most exciting thing at the moment in the young actors' lives.

At one point during the evening Dan asked Lee if she was working on a new play, and she told them about *Entrapment,* the two-character play she was completing.

"Have you had a reading of it yet?" Nonie asked her.

"I never even had a reading of *Alekos* before this morning," she admitted to them.

"You really should, you know," said Dan. "It can be very helpful hearing your work read aloud. Shows you where you're going wrong, where you need to revise. Lots of plays sound awfully good when read as literature, but don't play well at all on a stage, and you can usually find those things out in a reading."

"I don't know who I'd get to read it."

Three faces turned to stare at her. Nonie was the first to speak. "You know us, don't you?"

Lee was surprised. "But you're working in a play. I wouldn't want to impose on you."

"Impose?" Richard asked. "Actors thrive on doing readings. Asking an actor to read your play could never be considered an imposition."

"Absolutely," Nonie agreed. "We're all hams. We'd act twenty-four hours a day if someone would let us."

"Well, if you truly mean it then. Yes, I'd love to have you read my play. Could we do it some night after rehearsal?"

They all agreed that they'd be more than pleased to read for her any night she wished.

"But there's only two characters and three of you," she said, hoping that one wouldn't feel left out.

"Don't worry about it," said Richard. "Dan and I can take turns reading the man's part. Or I can read act one and he can read act two."

"And we can get Christie to share the reading with Nonie," said Dan with a straight face, then ducked when Nonie acted like she was going to throw her glass of beer at him.

At eleven they decided they better get some sleep since the next day's rehearsal was going to be early. Nonie and Dan took the same subway uptown, and Richard, who lived in Chelsea, not far from Lee, said he'd take her home.

Lee was delighted when Richard led her down a subway entrance, telling him she'd never ridden on one and how Paul seemed to be paranoid about them.

"A lot of people are paranoid about them," Richard explained, laughing, "particularly those who have been mugged while riding them. We poor actors can't afford taxis, though, like some successful directors can."

Lee didn't know what the fuss was about. The subway station was well lighted and full of people, and even though there was a man sleeping off a drunk on one of the subway seats, she didn't think it any cause for alarm. And it was a very quick mode of transportation; they were in the Village in less than ten minutes.

When they reached Paul's apartment, Lee asked Richard if he wanted to come in for some coffee. He refused, saying he wanted to go over his lines a couple of times before going to bed.

"Not that I don't like your company," he told her candidly, his dark eyes gleaming. "In fact, if you weren't the playwright and me but a lowly actor . . ."

"What?" asked Lee.

"I'd like to take you out," he admitted, sitting beside her on the front stoop.

"Aren't actors allowed to go out with playwrights?"

He thought about that for a moment. "I really don't know. I've never worked with a female playwright before."

"Don't male playwrights go out with actresses?" asked Lee, thinking about Paul's former wife running off with a playwright.

He laughed. "I'm sure they do. Does that mean you'll go out with me?"

Lee hesitated, wondering why she had led him into asking that question. She liked him a great deal. There wasn't the physical attraction with him that she felt with Paul, but he was far more pleasant company and she certainly didn't get tired of looking at him.

"I've embarrassed you," he said. "Forget I asked."

"I'm not embarrassed," Lee protested. "And yes, I would like to go out with you. I think, though, we should wait until the play opens."

He lifted an eyebrow. "Will you go out with me if it isn't a hit?"

"I hadn't thought about it not being a hit," she said truthfully. "I guess I should start being more realistic."

"I admire your optimism," he said. "I *never* think a play

I'm in is going to be a hit. I guess I don't want to jinx it by complacency."

"Anyway, I'll go out with you whether it's a hit or not," she promised him.

He stood up to go. "I'll hold you to that," he said, reaching out for her hand and pulling her up. He was looking down at her, their faces only inches apart, when Paul strolled up to the building and paused when he saw them in the shadows.

"Out rather late, aren't you, Jesse?" he said to the actor. "You have an early call tomorrow, you know."

"Yes, sir," said Richard, letting go of Lee's hand. "Good night, sir, good night, Lee."

Paul had stormed into the apartment, slamming the door behind him, before Lee had even said good night to Richard.

"He sure seems to be in a bad mood," Richard murmured.

"I seem to affect him that way," said Lee, wondering what kind of a confrontation she would have with Paul when she went inside.

As it turned out, there was no confrontation at all. The door to the den was closed as she passed it, so she went upstairs and got into bed. Which was just as well, she thought. She didn't know what to do about her feelings about Paul and his feelings about his former wife, but she didn't want to be forced into a decision about it quite so soon.

She lay sleepless for a long time, wondering about Paul, about whether she should remain as his guest in his apartment or whether she should find somewhere else to stay, although she wasn't sure she could afford anywhere else. At one point she heard him in the kitchen, slamming the refrigerator door, and wondered if he had had time to eat dinner that night. But knowing his propensity for food, she was sure he had.

She tried thinking about Richard too, trying her best to

summon up some romantic feelings for him, but it just didn't work. For better or worse, it was Paul she was feeling romantic about, and no one else.

CHAPTER ELEVEN

On Tuesday, after ignoring Lee the entire day, Paul handed her a small envelope before the end of the afternoon rehearsal and told her to look inside.

The envelope contained two tickets to one of the hit plays on Broadway and Lee lifted delighted eyes to him. "Are we going?"

"If you're interested."

"Interested! I've never been to a Broadway play in my entire life! Of course I'm interested."

He was trying to mask his pleasure. "I thought you might like to see it. A friend of mine directed it and we're meeting afterward for drinks."

He dismissed the actors at six and they walked back to the apartment to get changed for the theater. He spoke to her about that day's rehearsal and for the first time admitted that he might have been mistaken about Christie.

"I've seen the girl do some good work, but I don't know. This part just may be too much for her."

"Were you thinking of replacing her?" asked Lee, trying not to sound too eager and put him off.

"I didn't say that," he equivocated, "but something's sure going to have to start happening with her soon or . . . oh, hell, let's just enjoy ourselves tonight."

They were in the lobby during intermission so that Paul could smoke a cigarette when Lee recognized Jackie Flannery with a surge of delight just a split-second before remembering that the woman was Paul's ex-wife. The lovely actress was wending her way through the crowd toward them, her much-photographed smile in evidence, her eyes riveted to Paul.

"Darling, how wonderful to run into you," she said to him, brushing her cheek lightly across his.

"How are you doing, Jackie?" He seemed disinterested, but Lee could feel the tension between them.

If anything, thought Lee, the actress was even more beautiful in person than on the screen. She had the kind of elegance Lee vastly admired but was too lazy to try to duplicate herself. Always looking perfect took a lot of time and effort, and for Lee other things in her life took priority.

"Wonderful," was Jackie's reply. "I seem to thrive in California. Oh, I know you New Yorkers think it's an absolute cultural wasteland out there, but it's just not so."

"This is Lee Masterson, Jackie," Paul said, introducing them. "A native Californian and a playwright I'm currently directing."

Jackie's interest transferred to Lee. "A playwright! I was sure you were an actress. Playwrights didn't used to be so pretty, did they, Paul?"

Paul gave a noncommittal grunt.

"It's a pleasure meeting you," said Lee. "I've always enjoyed your work."

"Why, thank you. As I'm sure I'll enjoy yours. When does your play open?"

"We just started rehearsals this week," said Lee.

Jackie sighed theatrically. "How I'd love to get back to the stage. It's such a wonderful learning process . . . I don't suppose there's a part for me?"

"It's already cast," said Paul.

"Oh, too bad. I did happen to hear a rumor, though, that you were having a bit of trouble with one of your actresses. That you might have to replace her."

Lee glanced at Paul and saw his look of outrage. "Well,

you heard wrong. We have a fine cast—not one is being replaced."

"Oh, too bad. It wouldn't have been such fun working with you again, darling."

"Tell your husband to go back to playwriting and have *him* write you a part," Paul suggested curtly.

"Why, darling, hadn't you heard? We're separated."

There was a pause. "Sorry to hear that."

"It seems he has this proclivity for young actresses. Now that I'm over twenty-five, I no longer qualify."

"Tom was never like that," said Paul.

"He is now. One of the disadvantages of California is everyone is either under twenty-five or desperately trying to be."

"If you're fishing for a compliment, I'm sure you know how well you look," Paul told her. "If you'll excuse me, I want to say hello to someone before the intermission is over."

He was rude in his haste to get away and Jackie stared after him ruefully. "I don't know how well you know Paul," she said to Lee.

"Not very well."

"He can be a very difficult man at times."

"I know him *that* well."

Jackie laughed. "Nevertheless, I made a big mistake when I left him and I've regretted it for some time now."

Lee felt a pang of regret. It was one thing to be in love with a man who was still in love with his ex-wife. It was quite another when it appeared there was nothing preventing the two of them from getting back together again, except maybe pride or just plain stubbornness.

"I understand he's still in love with you," said Lee, then instantly regretted saying it. The last thing she wanted to do was play matchmaker with the man she loved and another woman.

Jackie's eyes widened. "Paul told you that?"

"Oh, no, he's never even mentioned he was married

115

before. No, it was someone in the cast. You know the way actors gossip."

"I know too well! I also know how young actors tend to romanticize things. Actually, when I saw you and Paul together, well, I thought perhaps you two . . ."

"We're just working together," Lee assured her.

"I see," said Jackie, and Lee thought the woman probably did see how it was. Lee was not very good at hiding her feelings; just because Paul was obtuse didn't mean everyone was.

The second act was ready to start and the two women took their leave of each other, Lee looking around for Paul. She didn't see him, so she went back to their seats and found him already there, staring stonily ahead.

He looked over at her briefly before the lights went down. "I used to be married to her."

"Yes, I know."

"Yeah, I guess it made the papers."

"No, one of the actors told me."

"Yeah, well, it's ancient history now," he said, but Lee didn't believe that for a minute.

Although she had loved every minute of the first act, the entire second act was just a blur to Lee. She found it unnerving having to sit in the darkened theater next to Paul, wondering how upset he was at having seen Jackie again. She had a feeling he wasn't concentrating any better than she was, and she longed to reach over and take his hand, but felt he would resent any efforts on her part to be understanding or to comfort him.

They went to Sardi's afterward, where Paul was to meet the show's director. To Lee's surprise the director turned out to be a woman, something Lee would have known if she had read the credits in her program.

The woman, Melissa Lamb, gave Paul an enormous hug and shook hands forcibly with Lee. She was a good-looking redhead in her forties, with curly hair and freckled arms, and Lee took an instant liking to her. Lee was also pleased to see that Paul seemed to be good friends with Melissa. Lee had thought he would have the same attitude toward women directors as he seemed to have toward women playwrights, but that didn't seem to be the case.

Melissa seemed as interested in discussing Lee's play as she was in the one she had just directed, and she listened with concentration to Paul's synopses of the play, occasionally interrupting to ask Lee a question and draw her into the conversation.

Lee was happy to see that Paul was acting animated, as she had been afraid the trauma of seeing Jackie again would affect him all evening. He did seem to be drinking heavily, though, but then so was Melissa. Lee decided New Yorkers as a whole just drank more than she was used to, and she just sipped slowly on a glass of wine.

They ordered thick, rare steaks, and Paul also seemed to have an appetite. Lee began to think that maybe she had been wrong about Paul's being upset at his encounter with his ex-wife, except that halfway through their dinner Lee saw Jackie enter the restaurant on the arm of a distinguished-looking older man, and she saw Paul pale when he saw the couple pass by their table without stopping.

"Well, well, so little Jackie is back in town, is she? I wonder what dragged her away from sunny California," said Melissa sardonically.

Paul ignored the query, and Lee, wanting to break the sudden silence, said, "Yes, we met her at the theater earlier."

"I'm surprised she didn't stop to say hello," said Melissa. "I directed her in her first play," she said to Lee.

"She didn't even see us," said Paul in a controlled voice. "Too intent on Miles Donahue, it would seem."

Melissa laughed. "Come on, Paul, you know Miles isn't interested in women."

"You know that, and I know that, but Jackie always thinks she's going to be the exception in every situation."

Melissa laughed so hard she choked on her food.

117

"You're right. She would see that as a challenge, wouldn't she? My God, she hasn't changed a bit. Looks good too. What happened to that erstwhile playwright husband of hers who went commercial? Have they split?"

"So it would seem," remarked Paul, then excused himself to go to the men's room.

As soon as they were alone, Melissa said in a confidential tone to Melissa, "You two an item?"

It took Lee a moment to realize what the woman meant. "Oh, no, nothing like that. Anyway, he's still in love with Jackie."

"Then he's a damn fool! Well, that man never did have any sense about women. I just thought, seeing him with you, he'd finally gotten smart."

"I liked Jackie," said Lee, not having any trouble understanding why Paul had fallen in love with the actress. Indeed, she was wondering why she had ever thought him attracted to her, especially after having been married to Jackie.

"Oh, sure, we all like Jackie. What's not to like? She's good to look at, she's always charming, and she's got a lot of talent to boot. But there's an ephemeral quality about her that, in my eyes, doesn't make her a likely candidate for a successful marriage. But that same quality is probably her biggest attraction for men, fools that they are."

"Did you know them when they were married?" asked Lee.

"Sure, I was at their wedding. Knew it wouldn't last too."

"How could you possibly know that?"

"Because I knew something Paul didn't know. Jackie was after Tom first, but he was involved with someone else at the time and just not interested. So she turned her attentions to Paul, Tom's best friend. I don't know; maybe she really did fall in love with Paul, but I was doubtful at the time. Not that he wasn't the better man, but who's being smart when they're in love? Anyway, Tom was

118

Paul's best man at the wedding, and even then, at the wedding reception, Jackie was playing up to Tom, batting those long lashes of hers at him, dragging him off on the dance floor. Paul was just real pleased she had taken such a liking to his friend, but some of us knew better. The two of them were such good friends. I think Tom spent half his time over at their place. Oh, well, it's all water under the bridge now."

"I'm not so sure," said Lee.

"Listen, honey, if you're interested in the man—and it would sure appear to me that you are—hell, you can barely take your eyes off him, then I say, go to it! You've got a hell of a lot more going for you than Jackie."

"Except that he loves her."

"Men always love what they can't have. He's probably been romanticizing her ever since she left him. If he could suddenly have her back, I think he'd get more realistic. Anyway, I think Paul's got too much pride to take her back after what she did to him."

"But if he really loves her, he shouldn't let pride stand in his way."

"Maybe he shouldn't, but he would—you can bet on it."

"He would *what?*" asked Paul, sitting back down at the table.

"Oh, I was just reminiscing about some people we used to know," said Melissa, with a wink at Lee. "So tell me, are we all up for dessert? Their black forest cake is just not to be believed."

Lee was distinctly uneasy during the cab ride home. Paul had started to put his arm around her, then, feeling her stiffen and draw away, had removed it, retiring to his own corner in silence. He had had a lot more to drink than she, but he seemed perfectly under control and she was very much afraid he was going to want to try once again to make love to her. She wanted to make love to him, which seemed only natural to her since she was quite in love with him, but she did not want to make love to a man who was in love with someone else. She did not want to be used as a substitute for the person he really wanted to be with, and that is exactly what it would amount to.

She glanced over at Paul, caught his eye, then looked away. Drinking obviously made him amorous; he never tried to make love to her perfectly sober, she reasoned. Maybe drinking made him forget about Jackie for a while, or at least dull the memories. Well, she was perfectly sober, her judgment not clouded in any way, and starting right this moment she was going to do everything humanly possible to forget all about this man—this lovely, sexy, desirable man.

She said a quick good night to him as soon as they got into the apartment, but before she could start up the stairs he had caught her around the waist and pulled her to him.

"If I didn't know better, I would think you were trying to escape my company," he said to her, caressing her back with his hands.

"It's late, Paul, and you called another early rehearsal."

"The director can always be late," he murmured in her ear, pulling her even closer to him.

"Please, Paul, I'm really tired," she said breathlessly, feeling the tingles all over her body from his touch.

He ignored what she said and leaned down to kiss her, a long, slow kiss that made her knees go so weak that she clung to him, returning the kiss against her better judgment.

He moved away from her and took her hand, starting to lead her up the stairs. "Come, Jackie, let's make love," he beckoned her, then stopped when he saw the look of shock on her face.

"What is it? What's the matter?"

"You called me Jackie."

He frowned. "I did? Sorry, a slip of the tongue."

"No, I don't think so. It's Jackie you want to make love to, not me." She felt tears starting and averted her face, not wanting him to see how much his careless words had hurt her.

"Don't make a big deal of it, Lee. Seeing her tonight and all—it was just a slip, no big deal."

"Yes, a Freudian slip," she muttered, trying to get past him on the stairs. He blocked her way, looking at her with concern.

"Don't tell me you're jealous of my ex-wife," he said, sounding disbelieving.

"No, I'm not jealous. I just don't feel like substituting for her, that's all."

He let go of her hand, a look of sudden comprehension on his face. "Oh, I get it. It's Richard Jesse, isn't it? You're using Jackie as an excuse, but that's all it is, isn't it? Just an excuse."

Lee didn't know what in the world he was talking about. "What has Richard Jesse got to do with this?" she asked him.

"Maybe if I had come home a little earlier last night—or a little later—you wouldn't be standing there looking so innocent. You think I didn't notice the way you two were looking at each other last night?"

"Are you crazy?"

"Sure. Crazy like a fox! Listen, you wouldn't be the first woman to fall for a good-looking actor—a good-looking *young* actor. Hell, enjoy yourself. He's probably a lot better lover than me—he's a hell of a lot younger anyway." With that he stormed down the hall to the den, slamming the door behind him.

Lee sat down on the stairs, waiting to see if he'd come back out and apologize. She didn't think he seriously believed there was anything between her and Richard; obviously he felt guilty about his attempt at using her and was trying to place some of his guilt on her. After she had waited several minutes, she realized he wasn't going to come back out, and she went upstairs to get undressed.

She looked at herself in the bathroom mirror and didn't

121

like what she saw. Tearful, unhappy eyes stared back at her. Her tan, which was fading from being indoors all day, gave her a paler look than she was used to, and she wondered that Paul would even use her as a substitute for someone as radiant as Jackie Flannery.

She suddenly felt homesick for California and wondered if having her play produced was worth all the unhappiness she was feeling at the moment. On an impulse she decided to call her parents in California. It was three hours earlier there and they would probably be sitting out on the patio, her father reading the newspaper, her mother busy on her latest needlepoint.

She sat on the edge of the bed and picked up the phone from the floor. Lifting the receiver, she suddenly heard Paul's voice, speaking low. She was too surprised at first to replace the receiver quickly, and, before she could do so, she heard a woman's laugh. A very sexy, enticing laugh. Lee hung up the phone as silently as possible, and crawled into bed. Quite unbidden, the tears started again, and this time Lee did nothing to impede them, but let the crying take over until at last, exhausted, she fell into an uneasy sleep.

CHAPTER TWELVE

The next morning Paul had the actors put aside their scripts and do improvisations. He told them that they were going back to the time right before the junta when Greece was still a democracy. They were college students —happy, carefree—looking forward to their graduation. A time when Alekos and Dora were in love and planning on being married after graduation. For Alekos, at least, the last period of happiness he was to ever know. He put them into different situations and let them make up the lines and action as they went along.

Lee found it fascinating. What astounded her, though, was the transformation in Christie. Without a script to weigh her down, she blossomed, almost took over the stage from the others. She was quick-witted, funny, and believable. However, she was not the Dora of the script.

After spending a couple of hours on the improvs, Paul took Richard and Christie through a difficult scene. Richard, as usual, was excellent, bringing an uncanny understanding of the character to the role. Christie was back to playing the "cheerleader" and Lee began to believe the actress would never improve. But if she didn't improve, there was the awful possibility that Paul might replace her, and that replacement just might be Jackie Flannery. Not that Lee didn't think Jackie could do justice to the part, but she knew that seeing Paul and Jackie in close proximity every day would break her heart unbearably.

On an impulse Lee drew Christie aside as they were all leaving for lunch.

"Christie, would you mind having lunch with me? Alone? I'd like to talk to you," Lee told her.

Christie appeared frightened, gazing at Lee with wide eyes. The others had all gone on ahead, leaving them alone. "Sure, Lee, if you want to."

"Christie," Lee asked after they had ordered, "did you always want to be an actress?"

Christie nodded.

"Never anything else? Even when you were a child?"

"When I was a child, I never thought about what I wanted to be. Then, when I got in high school, people would say to me that I should be an actress because I was so pretty. So I tried out for a play and found out that not only did I seem to have a talent for it, but I really loved it. You might not believe it, Lee, but I was pretty shy as a child. Acting really brought me out of myself—gave me some self-confidence."

Lee remembered having had students like Christie. Pretty girls who shouldn't have had a worry in the world, but for some inexplicable reason lacked any confidence in themselves.

"Christie, what would you have done if, after college, you were prevented from being an actress for some reason?"

"I would have died."

"No, seriously. Think about it a minute. How would that have affected you?"

Christie's salad and Lee's steak sandwich arrived. Lee began to eat as she waited for Christie's reply.

"That was my only hope, Lee. My one chance of getting out of that small Texas town we lived in. I think if that had happened, all of the meaning would have gone out of my life."

Lee nodded. "What would you have done about it?"

"I don't honestly know. Tried to find another interest,

I guess. Acting was so important to me, such a big part of my life, I would have had to find something to fill the void."

"That's what happened to Dora, Christie. She had always wanted to be a lawyer, was two months away from it when the Colonels took power. And to make things worse, the man she loved turned away from her at the same time."

"I didn't realize that," said Christie, so engrossed in what Lee was saying that she hadn't even begun to eat.

"I know, that's why I wanted to talk to you. The important thing to remember is that while Dora was probably a lot like you in college, she's totally different at the time in which the play is set. First of all, she's become a militant, dogmatic Communist. Do you know what that means?"

"I know what communism is."

"Have you ever known a Communist?"

Christie shook her head.

"Well, the most important thing about them to remember is that they don't have a sense of humor. Have you ever known a person with absolutely no sense of humor?"

"My father," muttered Christie.

"What?"

"My father has no sense of humor."

Lee, a bit nonplussed by this observation, encouraged the girl to go on. "Tell me about your father."

"Well, first of all, he's a Baptist minister. A Southern Baptist minister. He was very strict, never laughed, and took everything in the Bible literally. He was horrified at my acting because I had to wear stage makeup. He would never allow my sisters or me to wear any makeup."

"Did he quote the Bible a lot?"

"Oh, all the time. He had a quote for everything. You know, Lee, he disowned me when I came to New York. Said I'd learn the wicked ways of the city."

The girl was visibly upset at her memories. "Eat your lunch, Christie, while I talk to you," Lee told her.

Lee explained to Christie how she could draw on the character of her father to use for Dora. How Dora should have the same characteristics: seriousness, lack of humor, impatience with those who were more light-hearted, dogmatic about her beliefs, constantly proselytizing. When she had finished, Christie looked at her in awe.

"You're wonderful, Lee, you've made Dora real for me. I don't like her so much, but now I understand her."

"She's not an easy character to like," said Lee, looking at Christie's untouched salad.

"Could I tempt you into a strawberry sundae?" she asked the girl.

Christie grinned. "My daddy would say sundaes are a sin."

"He'd be right," Lee chuckled.

"You can tempt me, Lee."

When the two of them got back to the theater, everyone was there waiting for them. Paul glared at Lee with narrowed eyes, clearly suspicious of her motives in going off alone with the actress.

Lee ignored him and took a seat in the first row. Christie went up to Paul and spoke to him quietly for a minute.

Paul looked around at the cast. "Christie has requested another run-through of the scene we rehearsed before lunch. We'll take it one more time."

She still stumbled over some of the words, but there was a vast difference between Christie's performance after lunch and her performance before. She finally seemed to be getting into the character of Dora. Lee wondered if the girl was doing an imitation of her father; her Texas drawl seemed to emerge at times, seemingly without intent. Surprisingly, it sounded right.

Paul kept glancing between Lee and Christie, clearly bewildered at what had transpired over lunch to change the girl's performance so drastically.

126

When the scene was over, Paul congratulated both actors on the good job they had done and Lee saw that even Nonie was looking at Christie with a new respect.

An hour later, when Paul gave the actors a five-minute break to use the washrooms, he came and sat beside her.

"I don't know what you did to that girl," he commented.

"I ate lunch with her."

"Maybe you should be the director."

"I was thinking along those lines myself," said Lee with a grin.

"I'll ignore that remark," Paul said generously.

"I gave her a lesson in method acting," said Lee.

"You're an authority, right?"

"I've read Stanislavsky."

"Well, whatever you did, it worked." He reached over to squeeze her hand and Lee shrank away from him.

"Still mad about last night?"

"I wasn't angry last night."

"You gave a pretty good imitation of it then."

Lee looked away from his penetrating eyes. "I would just prefer keeping our relationship on a professional basis, that's all," she said, forcing the words out of her with an effort.

He let out a long sigh and stood up. "You women are all alike, aren't you? Never can make up your minds what it is you want. Well, I know what I want, Lee, and I don't give up so easily." He went back up on the stage as the actors returned.

I know what you *want,* thought Lee. *Sex. That's all, just some nice, convenient sex. And when you don't get it, you call up some other woman.* She felt herself getting tearful again, something that seemed to be becoming a habit, and left the theater to take a short walk and calm down. When she got outside, she met Frank coming in.

"How's it going, Lee?" he asked her.

"Pretty good, I think."

"You know what? You're beginning to look like a New Yorker."

Lee looked down at her jeans.

"I don't mean your clothes, I mean you're losing your tan. You're beginning to take on that pallor we theater folks have."

"Is there a beach around here?" Lee asked him, joking.

"No, but you can use the roof of the theater if you want."

"The roof?"

"Sure, that's how we New Yorkers get a tan. In the summer, the rooftops of New York are crowded with sunbathers. Also the fire escapes."

Lee wasn't sure if he was kidding her or serious, but laying out on a roof in a bathing suit didn't really appeal to her. Actually, working on a tan didn't appeal to her. She got hers because she ran on the beach every day in the summer, often participating in a volleyball game along the way. Just sitting on the sand doing nothing bored her silly.

"Have you met the costume designer yet?" Frank asked her.

Lee shook her head.

"Well, come inside. She's at work now and you can look at the sketches."

Lee followed him back inside and upstairs to one of the empty rooms where a young woman was busy at a drawing table. She looked up when they entered.

"This is the playwright, Gwen," said Frank, introducing them to each other.

"I'm really glad to see you," said Gwen. "I liked your concept of the black and white in act one and I'm utilizing it. Take a look."

Lee looked at the sketches, liking what she saw. The men, with the exception of Alekos, all wore black trousers and short-sleeved white shirts. The women were dressed in black skirts and white blouses. Only Alekos was different, all in black. Then she looked at the sketches for act

128

two, where Gwen had had to do research on the uniforms the Greek Colonels had worn.

"They're perfect," said Lee, and Gwen looked pleased at the praise. "In fact the whole production is going to be perfect, I think. The sets are great too—have you seen them?"

"Yes, Carter and I got together before we started. We liked the idea of keeping any color in the sets or costumes down to a minimum. We thought it would show, in a symbolic way, the drabness of the Colonels' regime, the dreariness of the life of the Greeks under the dictatorship."

Lee spent a little time watching Gwen at work before going back to the rehearsal, which was progressing well. When they broke for the day, Paul once again was meeting with the crew, and Lee went out for coffee with Nonie and Dan and Richard.

"What are you doing tonight, Lee?" Richard asked her when they were paying the check.

"I don't know. Maybe there's a ballgame on TV."

"Would you like us to read your play for you tonight? Sometimes it's good to take a break from the play you're rehearsing and do something entirely different. I'm assuming it *is* different."

"Oh, yes, this one's supposed to be a comedy—a romantic comedy."

None of them had anything to do that night, so Lee took them home with her. She told them to make themselves at home while she went upstairs to get her copy of the play. When she returned, she found them in the living room, looking around in amazement.

"This is the weirdest room I've ever seen," was Nonie's comment.

"Actually," said Dan, "it would make a great set. For something like *Arsenic and Old Lace.*"

Richard didn't say anything. He just walked around, pausing to look at all the junk piled everywhere. "I like it," he said at last. "It reminds me of my Aunt Martha's house in Spring Lake, Michigan. She's the eccentric in the family —hasn't thrown anything out in twenty-five years."

Nonie was laughing. "For your eccentric Aunt Martha, okay, I can understand it. But for a bachelor pad? No wonder his wife left him."

"I don't think it was because of the living room," Lee said.

"You never know," said Nonie. "What's the rest of the place like?"

"Quite normal," said Lee, then started to giggle. "Except for the sheets in the bedroom—they're lime green with purple butterflies. And that's in the strictest confidence, all of you. I really shouldn't have told you that."

"Oh, that's okay. I don't think the sheets are his fault," said Nonie. "I remember reading an article about Jackie Flannery in a movie magazine that said her bedroom in Hollywood was all in lime green and purple, so they're probably just a souvenir of the past."

Lee thought she'd rather have believed the sheets were just Paul's bad taste in decorating rather than know she had been sleeping on Jackie's sheets since she had been staying there.

They decided to do the reading in the kitchen, and Dan and Richard went out and came back with a couple of pizzas and some beer, and they all ate before starting the reading.

Lee's play, *Entrapment,* was about a rising young business executive, Ariel Ryan, and an educated young locksmith, Vinnie Domino, and their meeting when Ariel's apartment was broken into. The humor of the play came from Ariel's liberated attitude about men and Vinnie's old-fashioned attitude about women, and the fact that they were attracted and fell in love nonetheless.

Nonie and Richard read act one, and halfway through it Nonie had a speech about how she only saw a man once because after that the novelty wore off and it was all downhill. She was just getting into the speech when Paul arrived home, and stopped at the kitchen door to listen. He had a curious look on his face as he listened to the speech, and when it was over, Nonie stopped and looked expectantly at Lee.

"Do you want us to continue?" she asked her.

"Don't let me stop you," said Paul. "What is this, a reading of your new play?"

Lee nodded.

"You certainly have some strange views," he said to Lee.

Lee got angry at this. "I don't write autobiographical plays," she told him curtly. "Why is it you don't attribute Alekos's views to me, but as soon as I have a contemporary woman speaking, you think I'm spouting my own philosophy?"

"Playwrights usually do," said Paul with certainty. "That's usually why they write plays—because they have something to say."

Lee was momentarily dazed. "Well, I do have something to say, but that doesn't mean I'm Ariel. Actually, I'm all my characters."

"I didn't know you were schizophrenic," joked Dan, and the laughter eased the tension.

"Would you mind if I listened?" Paul asked Lee.

"No, not at all," she told him, not quite truthfully. She had a feeling he wasn't going to like the play very much, but it seemed rude to tell him he couldn't hear it.

"Have you eaten?" asked Richard, and when Paul said no, he got the last remains of the pizza and a can of beer. Paul dragged in an extra chair from the living room, and the actors decided to start again at the beginning for his benefit.

The play had some very funny lines, and the actors kept breaking up in spite of themselves, with even Paul unable to control his laughter at times. Lee was feeling very good about the reading. She had thought some of the lines were

131

funny, but the actors' delivery made some lines she hadn't thought were funny funny just by virtue of the way they read them.

Act one was practically all comedy. Act two got more serious, with the young couple slowly falling in love, knowing full well that they had nothing in common and diametrically opposed views on almost everything. In the end, although Vinnie is the first man Ariel has ever really loved, she says good-bye to him, deciding that her career means more to her than love. It was a poignant moment, and the actors read it beautifully.

Paul looked pretty shocked at the ending, as did Dan and Richard to lesser degrees. Only Nonie was thrilled with it.

"I love it," she told Lee. "It's so different from the way plays usually end."

"Particularly romantic comedies," said Dan drolly.

"Yes," agreed Richard, "you kind of expect romantic comedies to end happily. That's what makes them different from tragedies."

"It's all a matter of opinion," said Lee. "I don't happen to think getting married is necessarily a happy ending."

"It's usually thought to be," said Dan.

"I don't see why, with the divorce rate what it is," insisted Lee. "Anyway, the two of them had nothing in common."

"But they loved each other," said Richard, clearly unhappy with Lee's thinking.

"You can love someone without marrying him," said Nonie. "I, for one, am more interested in my career right now. Even if I fall in love, there's no way I'm getting married. Unless, of course, he's a producer," she said, reconsidering.

"Is that the way you feel, Lee?" asked Paul, looking at her intently.

"I just think it's time a romantic comedy got realistic," she told him.

He stared at her a moment, then said good night to them all and excused himself.

When he was gone, Nonie giggled nervously. "I don't think he likes your philosophy, Lee," she said.

"It's not a question of philosophy," insisted Lee. "It's just that I don't think endings have to be so predictable. I wanted this to be different."

"But will the audience like it?" asked Dan. "A good portion of the theater audience in New York is comprised of married couples from the suburbs. They like predictable endings—and that means marriage."

"I just think plays have got to get more realistic," said Lee. "I'm not writing a sit-com for TV, you know."

"That's for sure," said Nonie. "They wouldn't let some of this language on television."

Except for the ending, though, the actors all agreed that it was a very funny, entertaining play, and they were certain Lee would be able to get it produced.

"And we hope you will remember us when you cast it," said Nonie, grinning around the table.

"I expect all of you to be in a long run of *Alekos,*" said Lee. "But, if you're not . . ."

"You really need actors a little more sophisticated than us for this play," said Richard.

"Yes, you really do," agreed Nonie, reluctantly. "Now you know who would be perfect for Ariel? Jackie Flannery."

Lee had to admit the actress would be perfect in the part. "And what about Vinnie?" she asked them.

"Al Pacino," suggested Dan, and Nonie almost swooned.

"If you're going to have Al Pacino play Vinnie, you've got to let me play Ariel," she said seriously. "I'd do anything to meet that man."

They all agreed they'd like to meet Al Pacino, and after some more discussion about possible actors and actresses for the parts, the three of them left, as Paul had called another early rehearsal.

Lee took her time cleaning up the kitchen, hoping Paul would come out and join her for a few minutes. She didn't want a replay of the night before, but thought it would be nice if they could discuss the sets and costumes over a cup of coffee. But he didn't come out, and when she went upstairs, she thought she could hear his voice speaking softly and wondered if he was speaking to the same woman on the telephone. She was tempted to pick up the phone in her room and find out, but decided that was really sneaky and beneath contempt, and, anyway, he'd hear her do it, so instead she got into bed with her play and did a few revisions the actors had discussed with her.

She thought, about an hour later, that she heard Paul leave the apartment, and she got out of bed and softly padded down the stairs. The door to the den was still closed, and aside from opening it and checking on him, and perhaps annoying him if he was in there, there was no way for her to find out whether or not he went out short of staying up all night and listening for his return.

She decided to go to bed and get some sleep. If he was out, that was his business, not hers, she told herself several times, and it was only with the greatest of determination that she didn't cry herself to sleep once again.

CHAPTER THIRTEEN

The next morning on the way to the theater Paul brought up the subject matter of Lee's new play. "What have you got against marriage anyway?"

"Why don't you understand my plays?" she retorted. "You think *Alekos* is a political play, which it isn't, and now you think *Entrapment* is a play against marriage, which it isn't."

"What would *you* call it?"

"I'd call it a realistic, modern play."

"What's realistic about falling in love and not wanting to get married?"

He was getting her so annoyed she no longer cared what she said. "I would think, with your experience of marriage, you wouldn't be so quick to defend it as an institution."

"Is that what you think?" he asked, an angry note in his voice. "Well, my parents happened to have a good marriage, as does my brother. And I didn't mind being married—it just didn't work out, that's all. But I wasn't afraid to give it a try, unlike some people I know."

"Are you insinuating there's something wrong with me because I've reached the advanced age of twenty-eight and I'm still unmarried?" She thought he had a lot of nerve to infer anything of the sort.

"I'm just saying I think you have a lousy attitude, that's all." He quickened his walk, and she ran to catch up with him.

"Well, I'll tell you something," she almost shouted, "I'm very happy the way I am—and that includes not being married!"

"Good! I wish you luck in staying that way," he shouted; then, hearing how ridiculous they both sounded, started to laugh. "Can we call a truce?"

"Until the next time, I guess," she muttered, certain they were destined to argue about anything and everything any time they were alone together for more than two minutes, or, more likely, two seconds.

The rehearsal went well that day, and they broke around six. Lee was upstairs taking a shower before they went out to eat, when she heard someone ring the doorbell. Dressed in her robe she went to the top of the stairs to see who it could be. To her shock she watched as Paul led Jackie Flannery past the stairs and into the den, an overnight case in his hand.

She dressed as quickly as she could and went downstairs, but the door to the den was shut and she could hear barely discernible voices coming from within. Then she heard silence, and she began to get worried.

An hour later, the door to the den still closed, she went upstairs, wondering what she should do. It was obvious to her that the two of them were having some kind of reconciliation in the den; she shuddered to think what kind it was. She felt miserable and rejected and totally unwanted, and the last thing she wanted to do was spend the night in the apartment with Paul and Jackie downstairs. What was even worse, he just might ask her to move her things down to the den so that they could have the bedroom to themselves. At this thought Lee burst into tears and threw herself on the bed. Why, oh, why, did she have to fall in love with a man who was still in love with his former wife, she asked herself, but consoled herself somewhat with the thought that it wasn't her fault, he had never told her he was married until it was too late.

Not knowing what else to do, she called information for Nonie's telephone number, then called the actress.

"Nonie, this is Lee Masterson," she said when Nonie answered the phone.

"What's the matter, Lee?" asked Nonie, no doubt detecting how upset she was by the quiver in her voice.

Lee quickly explained the situation to Nonie, who was instantly sympathetic.

"You're right, you've got to get out of there," Nonie told her. "I have a couch that folds out into a bed, if you don't mind sleeping on that."

"I wouldn't mind at all," Lee assured her.

"Richard's over here—we were running through our lines together. Why don't we come over there, get you, and then come back here. How long will it take you to pack?"

"Two minutes."

Nonie laughed. "Well, it will take us at least a half hour. I live all the way up on Eighty-fifth Street. Just get packed and sit tight. We'll be there as quickly as we can."

Lee hung up and began to get her clothes out of the closet and into her suitcase. When she was done packing, she stripped the sheets and put them into the hamper, but couldn't find another set to put on the bed. Well, that would be Jackie's problem, she told herself, the thought bringing new tears to her eyes. She had never been the tearful type before and was beginning to wonder if New York was having an adverse effect on her nervous system.

When a half hour had passed, she took her suitcase and crept silently down the stairs and waited in the entry hall. There was still no noise coming from the den, which made her feel something like a peeping Tom, although it was listening she was doing, not watching.

The doorbell rang, and Lee admitted Nonie and Richard. They were just leaving, the suitcase in Richard's hand, when Paul, looking rather disheveled, came out of the den to see what the noise was about.

137

"What's going on here?" he asked Lee, looking as though he resented being disturbed.

"I'm not staying here anymore," Lee told him, fixing her eyes on his shoulder.

"You're what??"

"I feel uncomfortable being here; I'd just rather stay somewhere else."

Lee could see that Richard and Nonie were embarrassed to be caught sneaking Lee out of their director's apartment, and she quickly followed them out the door before she and Paul could get into a real argument. Quite by accident, the door slammed behind her, but she didn't think Paul would even notice. He was no doubt already back in the den, breaking the good news to Jackie that they had the place all to themselves.

Nonie had a small but charmingly decorated studio apartment with a small kitchen and a large, old-fashioned bathroom, complete with tub on clawed feet.

Lee walked over to the piano Nonie had standing in one corner, and played a short rendition of "Chopsticks." "Do you play, Nonie?" she asked.

"I accompany myself, not very well. I take singing lessons, though, and it helps."

Lee found that both Nonie and Richard took not only singing lessons, but also dancing, as did most other actors they knew. They also enrolled in acting classes when they weren't working.

"You have to keep perfecting your craft," Richard told her, "or you get rusty. I'm thinking of signing up for a class in mime next."

They were serious about studying their lines that evening, and Lee was allowed to read all the other parts while they learned theirs. It was fun for her, something she had never done before.

"I'm enjoying this—maybe I'll take up acting," Lee said to them when they stopped for a short break.

"I'd stick to playwriting," Richard joked, but Nonie

disagreed, saying that at least she read better than Christie.

"Well, I should be able to read it. I wrote it, after all," Lee pointed out.

When Richard had left for the night, and Nonie had settled Lee on the couch, Lee confessed to Nonie her feelings about Paul and what had transpired.

"Oh, Lee, that's so sad," said Nonie sympathetically. "But it's good you put a stop to it now. I kind of thought you two had something going, but it was hard to tell the way you fought all the time."

"That was part of the fun," admitted Lee. "I think getting along with a man all the time would become boring very quickly. I like a little adversity."

"Well, Jackie's more adversity than you need."

"That's for sure. One thing's bothering me though, Nonie."

"What's that?"

"Well, I think I really do love Paul, but if I *really* did, I figure I'd want him to be happy, and if being happy means him being with Jackie, then that's what I'd want. Only I don't want that. I wish that woman would just disappear and leave him alone."

"There's no need to be too altruistic," said Nonie thoughtfully. "After all, she hurt him once; there's a good chance she'd do it to him again. I personally think you'd be a lot better for him."

"So do I, but that's just speaking selfishly. Actually, when I met her I liked her a lot."

"Well, you're better looking than she is, and a lot nicer."

"Oh, come on, Nonie, Jackie's beautiful!"

"I don't think you have any idea how good you look," Nonie told her. "The only difference between the way you look and the way Jackie looks is that she works hard at it and you don't even bother. Anyway, you're a lot more talented. I think you're a great playwright, but she's only a mediocre actress."

Deciding that Nonie was prejudiced in her favor and also trying to make her feel better, Lee changed the subject. But the next subject not being nearly so interesting to them as the previous one, they both soon fell asleep.

The next morning they arrived at the theater at the same time as Richard, and Lee and Richard went inside while Nonie ran around the corner to get a dozen donuts for them to share. Paul was onstage talking to the stage manager about the props they would need and turned around when Lee and Richard came in. The look he gave her was so scathing she felt her knees go weak, and she took a seat while Richard went onstage. She didn't understand why he would look at her like that; she had thought he would be pleased that she had had the good manners to afford him and Jackie some privacy. She should have known never to get mixed up emotionally with someone she had to work with. Now here they were, stuck with having to work together during the duration of the play, and it was going to be difficult just to talk to him, let alone work with him.

He wasn't too annoyed with her she noticed, however, to appear immediately by her side the minute Nonie arrived with the donuts.

Taking one from the bag without even having it offered to him, he sat down beside Lee. "Listen, Masterson, there's one thing I think we better get straight."

"Okay," she mumbled, her mouth full of donut.

"We've got to work together," he said, his thinking obviously being along the same track as hers, "and for the sake of the play, we've got to keep personal feelings out of it."

"I agree. Is that all?"

"No, that's not all," he said, quickly swallowing the remains of his donut and reaching for a second one. "A few revisions occurred to me last night that I think we ought to discuss."

"When did you have time—"

"I found the time," he said, giving her a distinctly nasty look.

"What are they?"

He settled down in the seat. "In the scene between Papadopoulos and the prosecutor. I appreciate your humor, but I'm not at all sure it's to the play's advantage to have the dictator be so funny at times. The trouble is, you almost get to like the guy."

Lee thought a moment. "Well, it's kind of like the criticism you had about Alekos being too perfect. People aren't just black and white, and I thought if I made him just totally evil, he wouldn't be believable. He'd be just a caricature. Anyway, some people must have actually liked him."

"I understand that. I don't want you to make him all bad, that's not what I mean. But if you make him the only comic relief in an otherwise serious play, the audience is going to love him. Because they love to laugh. Do you see what I mean?"

Lee did see what he meant and agreed with him, but hated to capitulate so easily. Giving in too easily went against her nature.

He looked over at her with a grin. "You know, Masterson, I can read that mind of yours. You agree with me, but you don't want to admit it because you're too damn stubborn. You hate for me to have the last word, don't you?"

"If I do, I've learned it from you," she retorted, and he laughed out loud.

Nonie, hearing the laughter, looked down from the stage with a smile. "Hey, Paul, are we going to rehearse or can we all go out for breakfast?"

He got up from his seat. "Everyone wants to be the director," he muttered as he went onstage, and the cast laughed, glad to see him in a good mood so early in the morning. He was usually a bear until about noon, when he would start to mellow and they'd all relax. But they all had such great respect for him that they put up with his moods, attributing them to genius, something Paul would have laughed at had he known.

Lee had thought Paul would end the rehearsal early that day in order to get home to Jackie, but he surprised her by instead keeping the entire cast there until almost eleven that night, the latest they had ever stayed. Some of the cast grumbled about it, as they had had appointments or dates, but most of them were eager to rehearse as long as it took to make the production successful.

When they were through for the day, Nonie said she was too keyed up to sleep and suggested they go to the Village Gate and hear some jazz. Richard and Dan were willing, so the four of them walked the few blocks to the jazz bar.

It was crowded and noisy. Lee was constantly amazed that wherever she went at night in New York, the place was full of people, and she wondered if anyone in New York ever stayed home at night and watched television or just went to bed early. It wasn't a complaint, though, as she was a night person herself. Most of the writing she did was at night and, if she had her way, she'd sleep until noon every day. Except for maybe running, she didn't think mornings were good for anything.

The jazz band was good, and Lee was coaxed onto the dance floor by Dan, who wouldn't take no for an answer. She considered herself an atrocious dancer, but after two beers she could at least move to the music, and Dan wasn't a whole lot better. Nonie and Richard, on the other hand, looked like professional dancers, but then she guessed they were in a way.

When a slow song finally came along, Richard asked her to dance. He held her close and once again Lee wished she felt the kind of attraction for him she felt for Paul, but it just wasn't there. Maybe it was his age. He wasn't any older than some of the students she had taught, and she had schooled herself to never think of them in any but a professional way. Not that that was difficult for her; younger men, for some reason, had never appealed to her. Maybe when Richard got a little older . . .

At one they decided they better call it an evening. Richard walked home and Nonie and Lee and Dan caught the subway uptown. Lee was beginning to feel quite at home on the subways and wondered at Paul's aversion to them. She also liked the West Side, where Nonie lived. She was only a block from Riverside Park, a good place to run, and the area was filled with writers and theater people. Also, as Nonie pointed out, the biggest and cheapest apartments in the city were up there.

They got into bed quickly when they got home, and Lee didn't allow herself more than a passing thought about what Paul was doing at that moment, before falling asleep.

CHAPTER FOURTEEN

The rehearsal weeks passed quickly for Lee. With nothing much to do in the evenings when there were no rehearsals and Nonie busy working on her part, Lee got to work on her idea for a farce about a young girl and a fortune teller. She knew it wasn't a good play, but it amused her to write it, and she did think it was funny. It turned out to be a one-act play, and needed some filling in, so, in moments when she had nothing to do, Lee wrote some songs to go with it. She didn't make up the melodies, but rather used well-known melodies and put silly words to them.

She had no intention of ever trying to have the play put on, but one night Nonie asked her what she was working on, and Lee told her about it. Nonie insisted on reading it on the spot, and Lee handed it to her, hoping it wouldn't lower Nonie's estimation of her talent.

On the contrary, Nonie thought it the most delightful play she had ever read and immediately wanted to play the part of the girl, Nellie. "Oh, Lee, let's have a reading of it. We can get Richard and Dan, and Christie for the fortune teller, Madame Zola, and I can accompany the songs on the piano. It would be so much fun."

It was still early in the evening, and Nonie insisted on calling the others right away to see if they could come over. Like Nonie, the others were all at home studying their parts, and they were all more than eager for a break. Within the hour everyone had arrived and shared the one copy Lee had for a first reading.

145

Christie was the biggest success of the evening, reading the part of the aging Madame Zola with a heavy Texas drawl, a scarf of Nonie's tied around her head gypsy-style. Dan was also pretty funny. He couldn't carry a tune at all but insisted on singing at the top of his lungs.

But serious Richard was the one with the idea that really broke them up. He said he thought rehearsals could use some livening up and why didn't they practice the farce and, one day after lunch, spring it on Paul.

"He might kill us," said Christie.

"I don't think so," Richard insisted. "He has a sense of humor."

"That's almost like mutiny," said Dan.

"I don't think I want any part of this," said Lee, anxious not to start another fight with Paul.

"He'll never know you wrote it," pointed out Richard. "It's totally different from anything else you've written."

Lee looked doubtful. "What if he asks?"

"I think he'll be too busy yelling at us to ask," said Nonie, and Lee agreed with that.

But once the idea took hold, it was like trying to stem the tide, and Lee finally went along with it, promising to photocopy the play for all of them the following day.

They all agreed to memorize their parts that week, then get together over the weekend for extensive rehearsals. If they thought they were ready, they were going to spring it on Paul on Monday.

"Do I get to direct?" asked Lee.

"Of course," said Dan. "We wouldn't want anyone else."

Lee was secretly delighted to try her hand at directing, and, after hearing the reading of it, she found the silly play amused her more than ever and she began to realize she liked writing comedy much more than she liked writing serious plays. Which wouldn't please Paul, she knew, as he really went in for heavy drama.

The next day Lee asked Frank if she could use the

Xerox machine, and he told her only if he knew what it was for.

She gave him a suspicious look. "Why do you have to know what it's for?"

"Because Dan already told me what you're planning to do and I want a chance to read it."

"I think this is blackmail," observed Lee.

"Not at all—I'll even help you out. When you're all at lunch Monday I'll set up the stage and even work the lights for you. I've been waiting a long time for someone to pull a practical joke on Paul. I'm going to alert the whole staff to be here to see it."

"Oh, Frank, I don't know if that's such a good idea."

"Oh, yes, it is. They'll love it."

"Just don't tell them who wrote it, okay?" she asked.

He looked amused. "If it's good, *I'll* take the credit," he promised her.

The four actors went through rehearsals the rest of the week with sly smiles on their faces, but if Paul noticed anything amiss, he didn't mention it. He seemed preoccupied, but whether it was with the play or with whatever was happening with his life domestically, Lee didn't know.

When, on Friday, Paul began to suggest that perhaps the cast should have a Saturday rehearsal, there was such an outbreak of protests from the conspirators that he finally gave in after telling them he expected them to work on their parts over the weekend.

They decided to meet at Christie's place to rehearse, since she had a loft with the most room to move around. They were all there at ten on Saturday morning, lines memorized and ready to go, and Lee gave them all the blocking she had devised. Some of it didn't work, which they didn't hesitate to point out to her, but since she was surprised *any* of it worked, she didn't complain.

The scene where Richard impersonated Madame Zola was the funniest of all. Wearing a flowered hat and a

147

shawl, his voice pitched an octave higher, he had the group in hysterics.

The only real problem they encountered was that despite all their coaching Dan simply couldn't learn the tune of the song he was supposed to sing. Richard kept singing it along with him, but he just couldn't get it. Then, as they went through the play for the third time, at the moment where Dan was to sing the song, Richard dropped down behind Christie's couch and started to sing it in a loud voice. Dan, realizing what was happening, started to mouth the words while Richard sang. The others stood in shocked silence for a moment, then started laughing so hard they were unable to go on.

"Oh, Richard, I love it!" said Nonie. "It's got to stay in—just like that. I've never seen anything so funny in my entire life."

The others agreed, with only Lee having misgivings. She wasn't sure just how much of a sense of humor Paul had. If they had to do it, they at least should try to do a professional job, she thought, and that didn't include Richard dropping out of sight behind the couch in the middle of a scene.

They rehearsed all day, and that night they insisted on taking Lee to see the Theatre of the Ridiculous, just a few blocks away from Christie's loft.

"You've got to see it, Lee, he writes stuff just like this."

"Are you saying I'm a ridiculous writer, Dan?" she asked him sternly.

"Absolutely," replied Dan. "This is the most ridiculous play I've ever worked on. It's also my favorite."

Lee thoroughly enjoyed the Theatre of the Ridiculous and was introduced to Charles Ludlum after the show, the man who wrote, directed, and starred in the plays there. Dan told him about the play Lee had written and the joke they were going to play on Paul, who happened to be an old friend of Charles's, and he insisted on being there Monday for the performance.

Lee thought the whole thing was getting out of hand. Next they'd be selling tickets. She had a good idea that Paul would take a practical joke much better if there wasn't an audience around to see his discomfort. But there was no stopping it now, and Lee was unusually silent on the subway ride home.

"What's the matter, Lee?" Dan asked her.

"Paul's going to kill me."

"I think you underestimate him; he's got a sense of humor."

"Sometimes, but not always. There's no guarantee he'll have one Monday."

"I swear we won't tell him you wrote it," promised Nonie.

"Too many people know to keep it a secret," said Lee, and neither of them gave her an argument about that.

They rehearsed again all day Sunday. Richard suggested they go down to the Village Playhouse and rehearse there, but Lee was afraid Paul might be there with the technical crew, and she wasn't going to take any chances. By Sunday night it was as good as it was ever going to be, and before they parted they all agreed it was the most fun they had had in a long time.

The conspirators were so nervous Monday morning they kept blowing their lines, getting a lecture about it from Paul, who wanted to know why they hadn't been studying over the weekend as they had promised. Finally, in exasperation, he called an early lunch break. It was Lee's job to get him out of the theater during the break so that Frank and the actors could get the stage set up. She had to keep him away until twelve thirty, something she wasn't sure she could do.

It had been a while since she had eaten lunch with him, and he looked surprised when she suggested it to him.

"Any particular reason?" he asked her.

"There were some things I wanted to discuss with you

149

. . . about the play, and we never seem to get a chance to talk anymore," she told him nervously.

He took her around the corner to Eddie's, one of his favorite hangouts, where the bartender placed a glass of beer in front of him without being asked.

"They have the best hamburgers in New York here," Paul told her, then proceeded to order them without consulting her. She decided this was not the time to start an argument.

"Well, what did you want to discuss?" he asked her.

"I think I'd like a beer," said Lee, trying to figure out what to say to him. Her mind was a blank.

When her beer arrived, he asked her again.

"Is it the courtroom scene that's bothering you?" he asked.

"Yes," she said, wondering why the courtroom scene should be bothering her.

"Yeah, I know what you mean," he agreed. "What do you think we should do about it?"

Not having the slightest idea what he was talking about, she shrugged. "I was hoping *you'd* know."

He looked thoughtful. "I'm not sure. I don't really think it's the writing."

Lee was relieved to hear that. "Oh, good, I was afraid it was."

"No, I don't think so. Why, did you have some revisions in mind?"

"No."

"I don't know. I'll run it through this afternoon and maybe we can pinpoint the problem. I have a feeling, though, it's the blocking. And the timing, I think."

She nodded. "Yes, I had the same idea about the timing, but I didn't think it was my place to mention it."

"Listen, I appreciate another opinion. After all, you're the author."

Their hamburgers arrived and they ate in silence. Lee tried to drag out the time it took to eat hers, but no matter how slowly she chewed, the hamburger was still finished in under five minutes."

"Ready to go?" he asked her.

"I'd like another beer," Lee told him, hastily finishing her first.

"I didn't know you drank at lunch," he remarked.

"I usually don't," she said. "I'm just awfully thirsty today for some reason."

He ordered two more beers and Lee hunted around for a safe topic to discuss. Nothing came to mind. She saw a phone booth in a corner of the bar. "Excuse me a moment, I want to make a phone call."

"Who are you calling?" he asked, then saw her guilty look. "Oh, excuse me, I didn't realize it was personal."

Lee hurried over to the booth and called the theater. After about twenty rings, Frank finally answered.

"Listen, Frank, I just don't think I can keep him here much longer. I've ordered another beer, but how long can that take?"

Frank laughed. "Don't worry about it—it's all set up. I'll be looking out the window for you, and when I see you coming down the street, I'll douse the lights. And, Lee, quit being so nervous."

Paul looked surprised at her quick return. "Wasn't he home?" he asked sarcastically.

She ignored his question and started to drink her beer. Now that she didn't have to kill any more time, she was sorry she had ordered it. Two beers so early in the day could very well make her high. On the other hand, she might be better off high to survive the afternoon's events. She started to drink it.

"As long as you're going all out with the drinking, would you like a cigarette with it?" he asked her.

"I'd love one," said Lee, surprising him.

"What are you so nervous about anyway?" he said, lighting her cigarette for her.

"I'm not nervous," said Lee, finishing off her beer. "Let's go, okay?"

He paid the bill and they left. Lee could see Frank's face disappearing from the window as they rounded the corner, and she hurried inside.

"What the hell," said Paul when he saw the theater was in darkness.

Lee grabbed his hand. "Don't worry, I can see," she told him.

He let himself be led down the aisle and didn't even protest when she pushed him into one of the rows, taking a seat beside him on the aisle so that he couldn't easily escape.

The lights went up and there was Christie, a middle-aged Madame Zola, having an argument with her nephew, played by Richard. Lee glanced around and saw that about twenty people were seated in the theater.

The laughs started early, and once started, they never ceased. Despite her nervousness, Lee found herself laughing so hard at the actors that tears were rolling down her face and she was sometimes doubled up in her seat.

As predicted, Richard impersonating Madame Zola was a big hit. Lee heard a bark of laughter from beside her and turned to see Paul laughing with complete enjoyment, one hand wiping the tears from his eyes.

But the coup was when Richard dropped behind the couch and Dan pretended he was singing the song. It took the audience about ten seconds to realize what was happening, that Dan's lips weren't quite in sync with the song, and then the howls of laughter burst forth. Lee so forgot herself that she reached over and grabbed Paul's hand, shaking uncontrollably with laughter, wanting more than anything to just be able to roll in the aisle.

When the play was over and the lights went up, the audience went wild with cheers and applause. Lee briefly hoped the reception for *Alekos* was as favorable as the one for her farce, then she was on her feet and up on the stage, hugging the actors while they clapped her on her back.

Paul followed her up on the stage. "I want to thank you all for the most enjoyable time I've had in a long time," he told them, a big smile on his face. I don't know which one of you wrote this—"

"Frank wrote it," Lee said quickly.

He quirked an eyebrow at her. "Frank? *Our* Frank? I find that hard to believe, Lee. Frank can't even write a letter."

Frank appeared from backstage. "I heard that."

"I've seen some of your letters, Frank," Paul told him.

"Lee directed it," said Nonie, hoping to get the subject changed.

Paul turned to Lee. "*You* directed it? My congratulations. I didn't know you seriously aspired to be a director."

"It was a lot of fun," said Lee. "Much easier than writing."

That was the wrong thing to say. "Much easier? Perhaps you'd like to take over the direction of *Alekos.*"

"What I meant was, it doesn't take any thinking," said Lee, once again putting her foot in it.

"No thinking?" drawled Paul.

Lee gave up. "Listen, Paul, it's the two beers talking, honestly. I didn't do any directing. I just once in a while told them to move somewhere, that's all. All of them knew more about directing than me."

"Don't worry about it, Lee," he told her. "With your talent for writing, you don't need to know about directing. Did you think I didn't know who wrote it?"

"What are you talking about," said Lee nervously.

"Oh, come now, give me a little credit. It might not be in the same style as *Alekos,* but I can certainly recognize that ridiculous sense of humor of yours. Hell, it's the same sense of humor *I* have."

153

Various members of the Village Playhouse came up on stage then to congratulate Lee.

"Have you ever written anything like that before?" John Melfi asked her.

"No, that's my first farce," Lee told him.

"Well, it was vastly entertaining, my dear. I don't know when I've had such a good laugh. Why don't you write another piece in a similar vein and we'll put on an evening of your farces?"

"Are you serious?" Lee asked him.

"Perfectly serious. What do you think, Paul?"

"If we liked it so much, and we're an extremely critical audience, the public would love it," he agreed.

"Can I direct it?" asked Lee.

"No, you can't," Paul told her. "I'm going to direct it."

"But you don't like comedy," protested Lee.

"I don't like bad direction either."

"Don't let Paul mislead you," John told her. "He's directed comedy in the past. And done it very well too."

"It's just that I don't often come across something I like this well," Paul told her. "How soon can you have another one written?" he asked her.

"In a couple of days," said Lee. Comedy didn't take her long to write. Once she thought of a funny situation, it just seemed to flow.

"A couple of days?" Paul sounded disbelieving.

"Sure, you should see her write," said Nonie. "She wrote me a monologue I needed for an acting class one night and it only took her fifteen minutes. My teacher loved it too."

"I think you've found a treasure, Paul," said John before leaving the stage.

"Do you have any ideas for your next one?" Paul asked her.

"Tell him about Joan of Arc," said Dan with an evil grin.

"Joan of Arc?" Paul repeated.

154

Lee looked a little uncertain. "I had this idea for a rock musical of Joan of Arc. It would start off with Joan out in the meadow with her transistor radio, tending the sheep. . . ."

"Transistor radio?" asked Paul.

"Yes, to drown out the voices. You know, the voices that spoke to her."

Paul shook his head, as though not believing what he was hearing.

"It's really a very funny idea," said Richard. "We were talking about it last night."

Paul looked at Lee in wonder. "Just get it written down and let me see it, all right?"

Lee nodded.

"And now," said Paul, "if you characters don't have anything better to do, I think we should get back to rehearsing *Alekos.*"

Frank quickly put the stage back in order while the stars of the moment divested themselves of their costumes. Lee went back down and took a seat in the audience, glad things were getting back to normal.

A man came down the aisle toward her and she recognized Charles Ludlum.

He held out his hand for her to shake. "I am so glad you invited me to see that. Aside from vastly enjoying the joke played on Paul, I want you to know that you are welcome to become a member of my troupe anytime."

Lee thanked him for the opportunity but told him that much as she enjoyed farces, she wanted to write all kinds of plays and not restrict herself to one.

"Good for you," he told her. "And I'll be here on opening night to see *Alekos.* Good luck with it."

Lee didn't get her farce on Joan of Arc done before *Alekos* opened, though. With opening night not too far off, the rehearsals were stepped up, and Lee and the members of the cast and crew rarely left the theater before midnight, with weekends spent on such things as getting costumes fitted and practicing getting used to handling the props, particularly the printing press that figured strongly in act one. Lee, who was getting very little sleep, began to think she wouldn't live through it. Once in a while she looked back at teaching with nostalgia, but in actuality she was loving every minute of it.

CHAPTER FIFTEEN

Opening-night day dawned and Lee was awake to see it. Now, when it was far too late to do anything about it, she was nervous about the play. She was sure it was terrible: unreal dialogue, unbelievable plot, poor structure, and anything else that could possibly be wrong with a play.

Nonie heard her pacing nervously around the room and woke up.

"Go back to bed, Lee, it's the middle of the night."

"The sun is coming up."

"That's what I mean—it's the middle of the night."

Lee stopped pacing and stood looking out the window. She couldn't actually see the sun because there were buildings obstructing the view, but she knew it was coming up because the sky was turning pink.

"I'm too nervous to sleep, Nonie."

Nonie groaned. "Have pity on me. If I don't get some more sleep I'll fall asleep onstage tonight. Then you *will* have something to be nervous about."

Lee was instantly contrite. "You're right, I'm sorry. I'll be quiet, Nonie. You get some more sleep."

Lee went back to the couch and lay down. She might as well rest, even though she knew she wouldn't get back to sleep again. She wondered if Paul was as nervous as she was. Probably not. He must be used to opening nights by now. She wondered if he was sleeping peacefully or up and taking last-minute notes to give the cast and crew. She also wondered, fleetingly, if he was sleeping alone, but the idea that he might not be was too upsetting to think about and she switched her thoughts to more pleasant ones.

The success or failure tonight might very well determine her future as a playwright. It would, in any case, most certainly determine her immediate future. If it got good reviews, she would probably be able to interest a theater in putting on *Entrapment*. And, if she didn't make enough money from the play to support herself, she might be able to get a job teaching playwriting at one of the city's colleges or universities. With a teaching background and a produced play to her credit, she was certain one of the schools would take her on. As for becoming a member of the Village Playhouse, no one had ever mentioned it to her as a possibility, so she supposed it was a closed group and not in need of another playwright. Particularly a female one.

But no matter what happened, whether or not the play was a success, Lee had made up her mind to stay in New York. She didn't think she could ever love anything the way she loved writing plays and being involved in the theater, and now that she was, she was determined to try to make a go of it. It would have been lovely to do it with Paul, but even without him it was better than any alternative she could think of.

Lee began to amuse herself by thinking up a plot for a new play. She thought she'd like to write something silly the next time—maybe a longer farce. She thought of expanding the idea of a girl who goes to astrologers and fortune tellers in order to find a way to meet her true love, the basic plot of the one-act play staged for Paul. One of the fortune tellers has a nephew who, when the girl is there one day, impersonates his aunt and falls in love with the girl. He describes himself to her as her true love, and then

. . .

The next thing Lee knew Nonie was standing over her, calling her name.

"I have to go down to the theater, Lee, for last-minute notes."

Lee sat up. "Give me a minute to get dressed and I'll go with you."

Nonie shook her head. "No, you stay away from there today. Anyway, I made you an appointment with Fernando."

" 'Appointment with Fernando'—it sounds like the title of a play."

"He's a hairdresser."

"Why do I need—" Lee began.

"Have you looked at yourself lately?" asked Nonie.

Lee grinned. "Do I look that bad?"

"Your hair could use a good conditioning, and Fernando is marvelous at that. I also told him to give you a facial and a pedicure. When you need relaxing, there's nothing in the world like a pedicure."

"The whole works, huh?"

Nonie nodded. "It's your big night, Lee, you've got to look dazzling. What are you going to wear?"

Lee shrugged. "Now that it's cooled off, I don't really have anything."

"Then buy something. Do you have enough money?"

Lee nodded.

"Good. Then here's Fernando's address. Your appointment is at one. I'll see you back here around five, okay?"

"Okay." Lee got up and went into the bathroom to get a look at herself in the mirror. Even with the dim lighting Nonie had in there, she could see that her tan was gone, she had circles under her eyes, and her hair was looking rather dried out and limp. The circles under her eyes she attributed to Paul; thinking about him had disrupted her sleep. The hair, though, was her own fault. She was glad Nonie had made her an appointment with Fernando. She wanted to look her very best on opening night, as it might possibly be the last time she ever saw Paul.

She only had two hours before her appointment and

decided she better get moving. His address was on Seventy-second Street, not far from Nonie's apartment, so rather than going all the way to one of the department stores, she thought she'd walk along Broadway and look in the boutiques for something to wear. She didn't like department stores anyway—too many choices only confused her.

A winter white would be nice, she decided, and maybe some red shoes. They would look cheeful and optimistic, two things she sure wasn't feeling.

She passed several boutiques and noticed the color for fall seemed to be purple this year. Not that purple would be so bad if she still had her tan, but without it she was sure it would give her a washed-out look. Gray seemed to be popular, also—another color that didn't do much for blondes.

Red shoes, however, did seem to be in style, and she went into a shoe store and bought herself a pair of bright red pumps, deciding that almost any color dress would go with them. While she was there, she got a red leather clutch bag to match. She thought it was getting to be a little late in the season to still be carrying her straw purse.

She went into the next boutique she came to. This one also seemed to be featuring purple and gray. She took a gray dress from one of the racks and held it up to her face in front of a mirror.

"Perhaps with a little lipstick and some blush," a saleslady suggested to her.

Perhaps with a *lot* of blush, thought Lee, putting the dress back.

"Do you have anything in a white wool?" she asked the woman.

"White? No, I don't believe so. White isn't too practical in New York. I have something though—a bit unusual—that would be lovely with your coloring." The woman went to the far end of the store and returned with a long-sleeved, sheer wool dress in a soft shade of khaki, holding it up to Lee.

"With your eyes, your hair—it's a perfect color for you. Not many people could wear it, I think."

"Would it go with red shoes?" asked Lee.

"Perfect—the perfect color! What size are you, dear, a five?"

"Seven," Lee told her, hoping she still was, what with the lack of exercise and all the eating she'd been doing.

As the woman had said, the dress was perfect on her, and Lee was very happy to have completed her shopping so quickly, so she'd have a chance to eat before her hairdresser appointment.

Fernando was a delight. He turned out to be a tall, slim, gorgeous Brazilian who had his business and home combined in a colorful loft.

"Darling," he exclaimed upon seeing her. "What *have* you done to your hair?"

"Not much," Lee told him.

"You've been out in the sun, haven't you?" he scolded.

"I live in California—at the beach."

"Oh, my dear, you *must* stay away from the sun. It's dreadfully aging."

"How old do I look?" Lee asked him.

He stepped back and looked her over carefully. "Umm . . . I'd say you're pushing . . . twenty-three."

"I'm pushing twenty-nine and I've lived in the sun all my life."

"It will catch up with you," Fernando warned her, while leading her over to his sink.

He worked on her hair for over an hour, washing it, putting various conditioners on it, massaging her scalp, and when he was finished drying it, it hung to her shoulders like a sheet of silk, looking better than it had looked since she was a child.

Fernando saw her look of surprise. "Oh, yes, I can fix it for you now. But if you don't start using some conditioner on it yourself, one day I won't be able to do a thing for you."

Lee swore to him she'd start using conditioner, and even purchased from him the brand he recommended.

He put an herbal pack on her face and ordered her to close her eyes and relax while she had her pedicure.

The pedicure was a new experience and her feet looked and felt so lovely when he had finished, she vowed to make a habit of getting one. The facial was also a success. The circles under her eyes didn't disappear, but her skin came out looking rosy and glowing.

Before she left, Fernando insisted that she drink a glass of carrot juice.

"It is very popular in Paris," he told her. "If you drink enough of it, it gives you a tan. A very orangy tan, to be sure, but nevertheless a tan. And without the dangerous side effects of the sun."

Lee was afraid she would gag on the dreadful-tasting drink, but managed to get it all down so as not to offend Fernando. It was the least she could do after he had made her look so good.

"Now you are all set for your big date tonight, no?"

"What big date?" asked Lee.

"This is not why you come here? To look beautiful for a man?"

"No, my play's opening tonight."

"Ah, an actress!"

"No, I wrote the play."

His already enormous eyes widened. "A playwright! Fantastico! I am an actor."

Lee looked around the loft. "I thought you were a hairdresser."

"Oh, yes, *now* I am a hairdresser, but I study to be an actor."

"You're very good with hair," Lee told him.

"Oh, hair, what is that? It is acting that my soul cries out for, not hair."

162

Lee could understand that, not being very interested in hair herself. After promising to let him know if she ever had a part for him, she was finally able to take her leave. She had been there for hours and was afraid Nonie would be wondering what happened to her.

When she got back to the apartment, Nonie was so nervous Lee instantly lost her own nervousness and became calm.

"Don't worry, Nonie, you're marvelous in the part. You'll probably steal the show!"

"I'll probably forget my lines."

"Don't be ridiculous. You've been off book since the first week of rehearsals."

"I'm going to go blank, I know it. As soon as I walk out on that stage, my mind is going to be a total blank."

Lee told her that if that happened she'd personally go up onstage and do the part herself, and Nonie was so amused at the idea of Lee acting, that she lost some of her nervousness.

"You want to get some dinner?" asked Lee.

"Actors never eat before a performance."

"What about playwrights?"

Nonie thought a moment. "From what I hear, playwrights throw up on opening night, so you better not eat."

"I *never* throw up," Lee told her.

"Well, there's always a first time."

Nonie did some yoga exercises while Lee showered and dressed in her new clothes. When she finally emerged from the bathroom, Nonie told her she looked fabulous.

"It's got to be a hit now so everyone will yell out, 'Author, author,' and you can go up on the stage."

Lee looked horrified. "I don't want to go up on the stage."

"Then you better hope it's a flop," said Nonie matter-of-factly.

"Would I be expected to say anything? Give a speech?"

Nonie shook her head in wonder. "You teach school,

163

Lee, you talk to all your students. What are you afraid of?"

"I get nervous on a stage," Lee admitted. "I'm terrible at making extemporaneous speeches. Anyway, the audience isn't like students. They're my peers—judging me."

"Listen, Lee, don't worry about it. You'll only be going up there if they like it. Anyway, Paul will be up there with you and he's never at a loss for words."

It didn't make Lee feel any better to know that Paul would be up there with her to see her make a fool of herself.

"Maybe I *will* be in the bathroom throwing up. That way I won't have to go up on the stage," Lee muttered.

Nonie went to the kitchen and poured Lee a glass of wine, returned with it, and insisted that Lee drink it.

"Come on, you need something to relax you. I can't drink before a performance, but there's nothing that says the author can't."

"Have just a little, Nonie, let's drink a toast to the play. I don't know what's going to happen tonight, but I want you to know I really appreciate your letting me stay here, and I really hope we see each other again."

Nonie poured herself a little of the wine. "Here's to *Alekos*—may it be a great success and make us all rich and famous."

Lee lifted her glass. "May you be toasted as the new Sarah Bernhardt."

"And you the new Tennessee Williams."

Nonie washed the glasses and put them away. "Don't worry about not seeing each other again, Lee. And you're welcome to stay here as long as you want. I've enjoyed having you."

"And I've enjoyed it. But I need a place where I can write. And anyway, since I've decided to stay in New York, I want to get settled somewhere."

"It's not so easy finding an apartment."

"Harder than writing a play?" asked Lee jokingly.

"Much harder," was Nonie's serious reply. "But I'll ask around—someone in the theater is always moving out to the Coast. Maybe you could get a furnished sublet."

"Well, that's really too much to think about right now," said Lee. "Let's wait and see what happens with the play."

They got their things together and prepared to leave for the theater. "And I'm treating us to a taxi," said Lee. "Opening night is no time for a star and a playwright to be taking the subway."

"Amen to that," said Nonie.

Everyone was at the theater already when they got there, some of them looking as though they had spent the night there. Paul was running around looking distracted and didn't do much more than glance at Lee and tell Nonie to get her makeup on.

It was two hours until curtain time and Lee didn't know what to do with herself. She went by the dressing rooms and wished all the actors good luck, then went out to the lobby to look around. Frank was at the box office.

"Did you take a look at the marquee?" he asked her.

"Oh, I forgot all about it," said Lee, going out the door to the sidewalk and looking up. In big letters it said, LEE MASTERSON'S ALEKOS.

John Melfi came up as she was looking at it in wonder and put an arm around her shoulders. "First time you've ever seen your name up there?"

Lee nodded, too moved to speak.

"It won't be the last. We think you have a lot of talent, you know. We expect to see your name around in lights for a long time to come."

Tears started to stream down her face and she lifted her hand to wipe them away.

John handed her a handkerchief. "It's pretty exciting, isn't it?"

"You just don't know," she told him. "It's been my dream for years, and now it's come true."

"Did you see your picture in the lobby?"

"*My* picture?"

"Sure, along with the pictures of the actors. Come inside and see it."

There was her picture along with a brief biography. She had forgotten they had asked for some 8 x 10 glossy photographs of herself when she had signed the contract. She had immediately gone out and had them taken, the first pictures she had had of her since high school graduation.

Frank came out of the office and handed her a copy of the playbill, and she sat down in the lobby and read it through. It had biographies of the actors, the director, herself, and several others. She read through them all, although she knew most of the information already.

John, who had been conferring with Frank, came over to her. "Would you mind coming up to my office for a few minutes? There are some things I'd like to discuss with you."

Lee didn't mind at all—anything to take her mind off the opening for a little while. And she wanted to find out what happened now that the play was opening. She didn't know whether she'd be required to stay around for a while or whether it was time for her to move on to something else.

John settled her comfortably on a couch in his office, then took the chair behind his desk. "Would you care for a drink?"

"No. I had some wine with Nonie. I don't think I better have any more."

"First night jitters?"

"I guess so."

"I wanted to talk to you before the play opened because I didn't want you to think that what I'm about to say was contingent in any way on whether or not the play gets good reviews. We are all in agreement that it is a fine play, and if the critics don't agree—well, they've been wrong

166

before. The Board had a meeting this week and we're all in agreement that if you're interested, we'd like you to become a member of Village Playhouse as one of its resident playwrights."

Lee was too astonished to do anything but sit and stare at him.

"Of course you might not be interested. The show could very well go on to Broadway and you might think our theater too small or not quite what you're interested in."

Lee found her voice. "There's nothing I'd like better than to stay on here. I'd love to be able to work with a group instead of just writing on my own, and I think this place is just perfect. Would you tell me something?"

"Of course."

"Was it unanimous? Did everyone want me?"

"Everyone."

"Even Paul?"

"Especially Paul. And he tells us you have another play finished that's every bit as good as this one."

"We haven't always gotten on so well," said Lee.

"It's a rare occurrence when a playwright and a director get along well. That's part of the business."

If Lee had been younger and less experienced, she probably would have fled New York when things hadn't worked out between her and Paul, and she never would have agreed to stay on with the Village Playhouse, knowing she would be thrown into constant contact with him. But she wasn't a silly young girl anymore and those things would just have to work themselves out. Her career was what mattered and she thought, in time, she and Paul could probably become good friends. Love didn't last forever, not when it was unrequited. And, working in the theater, she was constantly meeting new men. Surely one of them would appeal to her as much as Paul did, or at least enough to get interested in. And, if not, she still had her writing, and that was a lot more than most people had.

Paul came bursting into the office at that moment and

sat down at the other end of the couch from Lee. "Am I going to survive this night, John? What do you think?"

"You ask me that every time a play opens, Paul. Yes, I think I can assure you you'll survive yet another opening."

Paul grinned over at Lee. "How's the playwright holding up?"

"Fine until Nonie told me that if it's a hit I might have to go up on the stage and make a speech."

"I've never heard you at a loss for words, Masterson," he teased her.

"You've never seen me on a stage either."

"Don't worry, you don't have to talk. You'll dazzle them with your looks."

"You do look every inch the successful young playwright," John told her. "You're looking especially lovely tonight."

Lee glanced over at Paul's jeans and ragged sweat shirt. "Are you wearing that tonight?"

"No, I have some clothes backstage I'll change into. If it goes well. If it doesn't, these are my suicide clothes."

"Lee's agreed to join our group, Paul," John told him.

Paul held out his hand to Lee and she took it. "Glad to hear it. I was afraid you would judge the whole group by me and turn us down."

"On the contrary, I think you're a wonderful director," said Lee.

"Yeah, but what do you know about directing?"

"I know you've made my play come to life. Made it look better than I ever thought possible."

Paul winked at John. "And she says that after a disastrous dress rehearsal."

"If the dress rehearsal hadn't been disastrous, I'd be worried," said John. "That's always a good sign."

"Is that true?" Lee asked Paul.

He nodded.

"Well, I wish you had told me that last night when I

was ready to run back to California and hide out," she told him.

"I thought you knew that—it's theater lore."

"Theater lore is still new to me."

"You'll get the hang of it," John assured her.

The lighting director came in with a last-minute question for Paul, and the discussion broke up, Lee going back down to the lobby in hopes of finding a cup of coffee before showtime.

Frank gave her a wink as she went into the box office and helped herself to some coffee from the always-ready pot.

"It's going to be a full house," he told her, "but don't take all the credit yourself. What with our season subscriptions, we seldom have an empty seat. Unless the show turns out to be a real bomb, but that's rarely happened, at least not since I've been here."

Lee looked out the window and saw a long line in front of the theater. "Why are there people waiting in line? Can't they come in yet?"

"They're hoping there will be last-minute cancellations, but for this one I don't think there will be. Hardly anyone ever cancels on opening night. They like the excitement of it."

"What do I do?" Lee asked him. "Do I watch from backstage?"

"No, you'd just be in the way. I have an aisle seat for you. I put you on the aisle in case you had to make a sudden run for it."

"I'm not going to get sick in there," Lee assured him, wondering why everyone thought playwrights had such weak stomachs.

"You say that now, but you've never had one of your plays open before."

"If you'd like to put money on it, Frank . . ."

Frank gave her a look of admiration. "I'll take your

word for it that you're the exception. The one playwright in all of New York with an iron stomach."

Frank reached over and began to blink the lights in the lobby, telling people that the play was about to begin. Lee got her ticket from Frank and found her seat in the already-packed theater, thankful she wasn't seated next to anyone she knew. She didn't want anyone watching her for her reaction during the play.

Despite the fact that there was no curtain, Lee felt a stunning thrill when the lights went up on the stage and the audience gave a burst of applause for the set. Christie made her entrance as Dora, the action began, and Lee felt herself transported into the Greece of the sixties.

The weeks of rehearsal had not been in vain. The actors acted effortlessly in their parts, nobody flubbed their lines, and Christie, who had steadily improved since her talk with Lee, took command of the stage. To Lee's mind she was still not the perfect actress for Dora, but she was a more unique Dora than she had pictured, and that might be even better.

The tension built onstage until the entrance of Alekos, about fifteen minutes into the first act. Lee thought she heard an intake of breath all around her when Richard entered, and she wondered if it was because of the plot, which had been leading up to that moment, or because of his devastatingly good looks. She thought it was probably a combination of both. He took over the stage like a dynamo, shouting, cajoling, doing everything in his power to persuade the other members of the Resistance to go along with his plan to assassinate Papadopoulos. His one long speech on the evils of the dictatorship brought an unprecedented burst of applause from the audience, and Lee felt tears come to her eyes.

The most dramatic occurrence in the first act was toward the end when Nonie entered as Athena and related to the group having seen her father, a noted newspaper publisher, tortured and killed by the Colonels' men. She noticed people wiping their eyes at the conclusion of Nonie's scene, and reached into her purse for a Kleenex to wipe her own.

Act one moved to a swift conclusion as the members of the group, one by one, finally agreed to help Alekos, and when the lights went down on the first act the audience was on their feet cheering and applauding. Whether it was for the play or because their own feelings of patriotism were aroused, Lee didn't think it mattered. She was on her feet applauding with the others, not sure it was good form for the playwright to be applauding her own play, but knowing it wasn't her play she was applauding but the wonderful performances of the actors.

The audience filed out into the lobby for the fifteen-minute intermission, and Lee followed them out. Drinks were being sold, and while Lee would have dearly loved to have something stronger, she settled for a Coke and went out in front to the sidewalk for some air. She noticed Gene Lesnek standing apart from the crowd and went over to say hello to him.

He looked surprised when she walked up to him, but held out his hand in greeting. "Didn't I see you sitting calmly in the theater during the first act?" he asked her.

Lee nodded.

"You must be an enigma among playwrights," he told her wryly. "Usually they are to be found pacing anxiously in the back, with an occasional quick run to the restroom."

Lee laughed. "Maybe I'm too new at this to get nervous. Anyway, I was thoroughly enjoying it. I thought they did a wonderful job and the audience seemed to like it, don't you think?"

He looked a bit uncomfortable at her question, but agreed that the audience had showed a great deal of enthusiasm.

"Listen, I'm not fishing for compliments," Lee assured

him seriously. "Anyway, you haven't seen the whole play yet. Personally, I like act one better than act two."

He looked amused at her admission. "Is there something wrong with act two?"

"It's not that there's anything *wrong* with it, at least I don't think so, but I just find the resistance group more interesting than a court martial. But that's just my personal preference. Actually, the court martial is pretty exciting if you like that sort of thing."

"Trial scenes must be difficult to write," he said.

"Particularly when they are nothing like trials in this country. I couldn't find any information at all on how the Colonels actually conducted their trials, so I had to make it up from scratch. The only facts I really had were that he made a speech about the tortures for the benefit of the Red Cross observers there, and, of course, the outcome of the trial. I don't imagine I'm spoiling the play for you by telling you all this, as you seemed to know all about Alekos when we talked before."

He laughed. "You're not spoiling it for me at all—it's nice to hear a little background on how you wrote it."

"With great difficulty," Lee said, laughing, "at least the trial part. "But I figured if *I* couldn't find out about the trials with all the research I did, no one in the audience would know any more than I did."

"Better hope you don't have a lot of Greeks in your audience," Gene chuckled.

"I hadn't thought of that," said Lee.

Lee felt somebody grab her hand and start to pull her away from Gene, and she looked around, startled, to see Paul, a furious look on his face.

"Come here, I want to talk to you," he said fiercely.

Lee gave Gene an apologetic look. "Sorry, I guess it's business. I hope to see you after the play. Maybe you'll tell me then how you liked it."

Lee could hear him laughing as Paul led her over to a quiet corner of the street.

"Why did you embarrass me like that?" she asked him, once again feeling herself becoming angry with Paul's behavior.

"Embarrass *you?*" he asked, a look of incredulity on his face. "What the hell do you think you're doing talking to Gene Lesnek? Don't you have any sense at all?"

"Why shouldn't I talk to him—we're friends. I'll talk to whomever I wish to talk to and I wish you'd quit interfering." She tried to pull away from him, but he wouldn't let go of her hand.

"Don't you know who he is?"

"Sure, he's Gene Lesnek."

He shook his head in exasperation. "Do you happen to know what he does for a living?"

Lee briefly wondered if that nice man was a member of the Mafia. "He told me he was a newspaper reporter."

Paul raised his eyes to heaven as though looking for help. "I can't believe how uninformed you are. He just happens to be the chief drama critic for *The New York Times,* that's all."

"You're kidding?" said Lee, delighted to hear that her friend was really interested in the theater.

"No, I'm not kidding. And I guess you also don't know what bad form it is for a playwright to be seen buttering up a drama critic at the opening of her play. Why didn't you just hand him a bribe, for God's sake?"

"You are being totally unfair," said Lee, raising her voice in anger. "Why would I be buttering him up if I didn't even know who he was. And furthermore, he *knows* I didn't know he was a drama critic. He, however, does not have your bad manners!"

Paul let go of her hand. "I swear to God, Masterson, you really need educating. Just do me a favor, okay? Don't talk to *anyone* without asking me first. I only hope he doesn't murder us in his review."

"Why should he do that? I think it's going beautifully. The audience seems to love it."

"Gene has not always been known to agree with the audience. And he sure demolished a couple of the plays I directed in the past."

"Well, maybe you've improved since then," Lee couldn't resist saying, then moved quickly back to the theater before Paul could yell at her again.

He walked by her on the way in. "Touché, Masterson," he murmured as he passed her, causing her to laugh out loud, then feel foolish as several people turned to see what she was laughing at.

Lee returned to her seat as the lights were going down. There was again the expectant hush as act two was about to begin.

The first scene, between Papadopoulos, the prosecutor, and the judge, went extremely well, Papadopoulos getting some laughs in his attempts to appear intelligent with the judge. The part was played by a well-known character actor whom Lee much admired. She hadn't gotten to know him very well, as he was a private individual who seemed to keep himself aloof from the rest of the cast.

The most dramatic moment came when Alekos was led in by two guards, tortured to the point where he could no longer walk by himself and had to be strapped to the witness chair in order to sit upright. His feet, a mass of open wounds, were bandaged, his long sleeves covered numerous wounds and scars, but his eyes burned as brightly and his spirit never faltered.

The play built slowly and inexorably to its dramatic conclusion, then paused briefly for a short epilogue wherein Alekos was seen in a jail cell, reciting one of the poems he had smuggled out; one of the poems that he had written in blood.

There was absolute silence for a moment at the end of the play, then the audience, as one, was on its feet, cheering, clapping, a few bravos being yelled out.

Lee liked the curtain calls Paul had devised. First the members of the Resistance, except for Alekos, came out

174

hand in hand. Then, from the other side of the stage came the "bad guys," Papadopoulos and his minions. Then, from center stage, came Alekos, joining the two groups together.

Many curtain calls were taken, Richard receiving the bulk of the applause, as was right, since his part far exceeded that of the others in both length and intensity. It seemed as though the audience would never stop applauding, and Paul finally took the stage, holding up his hands for quiet.

"Thank you," he said to the audience, "for what we hope is another successful opening to another successful season. It's good to see so many familiar faces here again, as well as many newcomers whom we wish to welcome. I don't intend to make a speech—"

He was drowned out by cheers and then laughter at that point, and there were shouts of "author, author" from the audience.

Paul held up his hands once again. "The author of tonight's play, as you will have noticed from your playbills, is Lee Masterson. Lee, will you please come up onstage?"

Lee found that she was too excited to be nervous about going up on the stage. She saw the people around her give her surprised looks as she got out of her seat and headed for the steps leading to the stage.

"This is Lee's first play," Paul was telling them, "and we at the Village Playhouse think she has a unique voice, and one that should be nurtured. It is my distinct pleasure to tell you that Lee has agreed to become a resident member of the Playhouse and we hope that you will see many more plays of hers in the years to come.'"

Lee had reached his side by now, and there was renewed cheering when the audience caught sight of the playwright.

"Lee, would you like to make a speech?" Paul asked her.

Lee shook her head and the audience laughed and then applauded harder.

"Isn't there anything you wish to say?"

Lee thought a moment. "I thought it was wonderful," she said shyly, and the audience again broke out into sympathetic laughter.

Paul took her hand. "Tell me, Lee, how are you feeling at this moment?"

Lee gave him a devilish look. "Hungry," she said. "I was told not to eat before the show."

Again the audience burst into laughter, Paul along with them.

"If she doesn't make it as a playwright," said Paul, "I think she'd have a good chance as a comedienne."

Paul led Lee backstage as the audience finally started to leave the theater, and she was surrounded by the cast, all of whom wanted to give her a congratulatory kiss and hug. She felt surrounded by the same warmth and love she had always received from her family, and felt perfectly at home.

"What do we do now?" Lee asked Paul. "Do we go to Sardi's and wait for the reviews to come out?"

"That's only for Broadway shows," he told her. "What we're going to do is go back to my place for a party . . . and wait for the reviews to come out."

"Do you have food?" she asked him.

"Give me some credit for managing to eat before you came along," he told her. "Anyway, the Playhouse is having it catered."

"Well, let's go, I'm starving," said Lee, and got her best laugh of the evening.

CHAPTER SIXTEEN

Lee noticed at once that a lot of the "memorabilia" had been moved out of the living room for the party, and the caterers had set up a fully equipped bar in one corner. There was a long table against one wall with a mouthwatering display of food, and Lee noticed that the cast seemed as hungry as she was, all of them piling their plates with food and ignoring the bar for the moment.

She found a seat by Nonie, and Richard came over to join them. Dan, she noticed, was sitting with Christie, and Lee suddenly realized she had seen the two of them together quite a lot lately. She asked Nonie about it.

"Yes, I think we have a budding romance in our midst," Nonie said, laughing. "An unlikely pair, but I think it's good for both of them."

"Romance is good for anyone," pointed out Richard, his eyes warm on Lee, and she wished she could return the look. It was too soon, though; her eyes still followed Paul's every move, much as she would have liked to ignore him.

"Do we wait up until dawn for the reviews?" Lee asked.

"No, nothing like that," said Nonie. "We should know the good news by midnight, thank God. I feel as though I could sleep for twenty-four hours."

"I'm glad to hear you say good news," said Richard. "But let's not get our hopes up."

Nonie looked up from her food. "Well, I've never been in a professional play before, but I don't see how the response could have been any better."

"But you've got to remember," Richard argued, "most of the audience was comprised of patrons of the theater. They probably support anything it does."

"I don't care what you say," said Lee. "All of you were so wonderful I don't see how it could help get good reviews. If anything bad is said about it, it should be about my writing, because the acting couldn't possibly have been better." Then, remembering what had happened earlier in the evening, she told them about her encounter with Gene Lesnek and how Paul had dragged her away from the critic.

Richard looked shocked, but Nonie thought it was hilarious. "Oh, Lee, I wish I could have been there to see it. You and Gene Lesnek discussing your play at intermission—that's priceless!"

"And foolish," added Richard.

"But I didn't know who he was," said Lee, defending herself.

"How could anyone be in the theater and not know who Gene Lesnek was?" asked Richard.

"Well, for one thing," said Lee, "I didn't read *The New York Times* in California. We have the *Los Angeles Times* out there, and Gene Lesnek doesn't happen to write for it. Anyway, he's a very nice man and I don't think he'll take it amiss."

Nonie was laughing. "I have never before heard Gene Lesnek described as a nice man, but I'll take your word for it. Anyway, it's in our favor if he was nice to you."

Lee kept looking around, wondering when Jackie Flannery would appear. She hadn't seen her at the theater, but was sure she'd show up at the party. After a while she began to think perhaps she wasn't coming. Maybe it was a closed party, closed except to the members of the cast and crew and Playhouse staff. None of the actors' friends or family were there, so maybe it was some more of show-business lore—no outsiders at opening-night parties. She thought that would make it rather awkward for Jackie, though, particularly if she was living with Paul. Lee had a sudden urge to go upstairs and check out the bedroom, but she just couldn't bring herself to do such a sneaky thing, plus there was a good chance she'd be seen doing it.

The theater had sent Frank and a couple of his friends to the newspaper offices with instructions to take cabs back with the reviews as soon as they were printed. Shortly after eleven thirty, the young man who had gone to the *Post* offices came back waving the review in the air, a jubilant smile on his face.

Everyone gathered around as he handed it to Paul. Paul looked over at Lee. "Would you like to read it?"

Lee shook her head, not wanting to be the center of attention and knowing that Paul was revelling in the moment anyway.

The *Post* critic was unabashedly enthusiastic about the play, questioning only a couple of the courtroom procedures Lee had used. Lee questioned them herself, and thought she had better rewrite what the critic found remiss. The praise was high for the actors, particulary Richard, but what really surprised Lee was that Christie was singled out for much praise and her casting hailed as "the most interesting counter-casting this critic has seen in many a season in New York." He said Christie had a "luminosity that lit up the stage." Lee looked over at Christie and saw that the girl was in tears of happiness, and she felt very proud at how far Christie had come in her part.

Paul brought forth a bottle of Dom Perignon, and they all toasted the *Post*'s review.

"Are you happy?" Lee asked him as he filled her glass.

"Oh, the *Post* is always approving of what we do," he told her. "The real test will be the *Times*, if you didn't foul us up."

"If there's some protocol involved," Lee informed him,

179

"Gene Lesnek was at fault, not me. I didn't invite *him* home with me for lemonade."

Paul, who hadn't known about that incident, demanded to be told about it at once, but even he could find no fault in her behavior that day. "You should have told me about it before," was all he said.

"I would have, but that was the day you came home and fell right asleep, and by the next day I had forgotten about it."

"He must not have made a very good impression on you," Paul chuckled.

"On the contrary, I find him very charming," said Lee. "It's just that we really haven't done much talking since then."

"That's not my fault," Paul began to argue, but then the young woman from the *News* came in with their review, and once again Paul read it aloud.

The *News,* if anything, had an even more favorable review. The review was entitled "Headed Straight for Broadway" and hailed Lee as the find of the season, the reviewer saying he hadn't liked a play so much since *Elephant Man.* Lee, who had never seen *Elephant Man,* didn't know whether this was as good as it sounded, but was assured by Paul that it was. *Elephant Man,* she was told, had been a huge success—both critically and with the public.

Dan came up to where Lee was standing with Paul. "Will you remember your old friends when you're rich and famous?" he asked her with his elfin grin.

"Am I going to be rich and famous?" she asked.

"If it goes to Broadway, you will. Won't she, Paul?"

"There's always that possibility," said Paul, not looking too thrilled.

"Does that mean I won't have to teach anymore?" asked Lee, thinking what a wonderful thing that would be.

"You won't have to anyway," Paul told her. "You'll get a salary at the Playhouse—didn't John tell you that?"

She shook her head. "But I guess he just didn't get around to it."

At twelve thirty, when the expectations over the *Times*'s review had reached a feverish pitch, Frank returned, and with him, Gene Lesnek. It was such an unprecedented happening that the room practically went into a state of shock.

John Melfi was the first to recover, going over and shaking the critic's hand with warmth. "I don't believe this has ever happened before," he told Gene with a twinkle in his eye, "but I want you to know I think it really shows guts on your part. You know, of course, we'll tear you apart if we don't like the review."

"I was assuming you were all civilized people," Gene quipped.

"Not *that* civilized," said John.

Gene looked over at Paul and Lee. "Do I get a glass of that champagne?"

"Not until we've heard the review," said Paul, but Lee poured him a glass and carried it over to him.

"Of course you do," she said. "And I want to apologize to you. I understand I behaved in a most disgraceful manner by being friendly with a critic. Of course, you could have told me just exactly what it was you wrote for newspapers. I assumed you were some sort of political writer."

"But I am," he said to her with a smile. "You'll find there's more politics going on in the theater than almost anywhere else. Wouldn't you agree, John?"

"This is no time for arguments," John told him. "For God's sake, man, let's have the review!"

Gene, not at all embarrassed by being the center of attention, put down his glass of champagne, held up his review, and began to read. "Dear Ms. Masterson," he began, "tonight I fell in love. With a hero, with a Resistance group, with a cause . . . in short, with the talent of a dazzling new playwright, an occurrence I feel honored to have been a part of. With a talent like this, the New York theater can no longer be said to be in any trouble."

It went on from there, praising the directing skill of Paul, singling out each actor with praise, commenting favorably on the set design and costumes, in short, finding no fault whatsoever with anything in the production. When he had finished reading, those assembled were speechless with delight.

Gene went over to Paul. "I hope you're planning on taking it to Broadway. It's the kind of play we've been waiting for for a long time. Of course, as you probably realize, it meant a lot to me personally."

"Personally?" Lee asked him, not knowing what he meant.

"Gene was a member of the Underground in Romania," Paul explained to her. "He was quite a hero over there. Get him to tell you about his escape sometime. In fact, you could probably write a play about the incident."

Lee looked at Gene with new respect. "Why didn't you tell me that?"

"I didn't want to take unfair advantage," he told her. "Anyway, I could see you were besotted by Alekos."

Paul laughed at the man's insight. "Exactly what I told her," he said.

"Then justifiably you should be besotted by the actor playing Alekos," said Richard, looking at Lee over the rim of his glass.

"You wouldn't even question that if you had seen how she fought for you for the part," Paul said to him. "Not that she wasn't right—you were superb—but I must admit I didn't think you had the experience to carry the part."

"I hope you remember that 'superb' when you're casting it for Broadway," said Richard, and there was general laughter.

A little while later Nonie asked Lee if she'd mind if she went home. "I'm exhausted, and we do have a performance tomorrow night, you know."

"Go on ahead," Lee told her. "I can get a taxi uptown with some of the others later." They kissed each other good night, and Nonie left, a few of the others following after her.

An hour later, when the room got so smoky Lee felt the need of some fresh air, she went into the den and sat down on the couch, thinking she'd rest for a few minutes before rejoining the party. The next thing she knew Paul was shaking her by the shoulder.

"Wake up, Lee, the party's over."

Lee opened sleepy eyes. "Has everyone gone?"

"Everyone but you. Come on, I'll walk you home. That is, if you can walk in those shoes."

Lee found the shoes comfortable enough, but found it hard to believe Paul was capable of walking such a long distance. He usually took cabs for anything beyond a few blocks.

She found her purse and a sweater Nonie had loaned her, and they left the apartment. It was a lovely night out, cool but clear, and Lee was glad that summer, with the dreadful humidity, was over. When Paul started off in the wrong direction, heading crosstown instead of uptown, she stopped him.

"That's the wrong way," she pointed out.

"I thought Jesse lived in Chelsea," he said.

"Richard? What has Richard got to do with it?"

He looked confused. "Aren't you staying with Richard Jesse?"

Now Lee was confused. "Why would I be staying with Richard Jesse?"

"Well, he came over that night and was carrying your suitcase when you left."

"He came over with Nonie. I'm staying with Nonie. Did you really think I'd just move in with Richard Jesse?"

"I thought you liked him."

"I do like him, but I don't move in with every man I like, you know."

"Well, how was I to know? I thought you and Richard . . ."

"We're friends, that's all," Lee told him, wondering at his sudden interest in her personal life. He hadn't spoken to her about anything except the play since she had moved out.

"You mean you're not in love with him?"

"No, not with him," Lee told him. Then realizing what she said, she started off down the sidewalk so he wouldn't see the blush she could feel on her face.

He went after her and swung her around, his hands on her shoulders, his eyes staring at her intently.

"I've missed you, Lee," he told her.

"You've seen me practically every day."

"You know that's not what I mean. I don't know what happened to us, but whatever it was, I wish we could straighten it out. Would you come home with me? You can have the bedroom. I'll move back down to the den, I promise."

Lee was becoming confused. "What about Jackie?"

"What?"

"Jackie. Your ex-wife. The one you're getting back together with."

"Jackie's in California. I don't know what the hell you're talking about."

"I thought she had moved back in with you."

"Are you crazy? You think I'd be that stupid a second time?"

"But that night she came over . . ."

"Oh, she wanted to give it another try all right, but I told her I was in love with you."

Lee was too stunned to say anything, but she didn't have to because Paul had taken her into his arms and bent down to kiss her. When he stopped and took her hand once again, it was in the direction of his apartment that he was headed.

"You really love me?" she asked, hardly believing what she had heard.

"Hell, yes," he said, speeding up their walk.

"Since when?"

"You want to know the exact moment?"

"Yes."

He stopped and turned to her. "It was when you threw your driver's license down in front of me. I suddenly realized that not only did you have that fantastic mind that wrote *Alekos,* and not only were you the most gorgeous woman I had ever laid eyes on, but you also had spirit. I like spirit in a woman."

"Do you know when I fell in love with you?" she asked him.

His face took on a happiness she had never seen there before. "I hadn't known you did," he said quietly.

"Listen, Paul, I don't go to bed with men I don't love."

"Well, it's not as though we did anything."

"We did enough."

"I guess you're right," he said, a fond look of remembrance on his face. "Tell me, when did you fall in love with me?"

"When you made me eat the veal scallopini."

"Not until then?" he complained. "I had been in love with you a good hour by that time."

"I'm just slower than you, I guess," she said, leaning close to him.

"No, not here. Let's go home."

"Have you had a lot to drink?" she asked him, remembering the first night.

"No."

"Will you take the phone off the hook?"

"First thing."

"Can we get married onstage?"

Paul looked shocked. "Who said anything about marriage?"

"Are you telling me you don't have honorable intentions?"

"I have honorable intentions, but I think you could have let me do the proposing."

"You really are a male chauvinist."

"Damn right! At least when it comes to proposing."

"All right, forget I mentioned it. I'm liberated. I'm not sure I want to get married anyway."

"You'll marry me, all right."

"What makes you think so?"

"No marriage, no sex," he said.

"Does that include tonight?"

"No, that starts tomorrow."

"Well, then let's go," she said, and they fairly ran back to his apartment.

The first thing Lee noticed in the bedroom was that the lime green sheets were gone. After that she didn't notice much of anything, as Paul's expert hands started to undress her. He didn't act with haste, but slowly and lovingly removed her dress, her slip, her bra, her panties and her panty hose, first having removed her red shoes. He then divested himself of his own clothes in record-breaking time, before pulling her down on the bed with him.

"Oh, God, how I love you," he said, his voice a soft moan, his face burying itself against the soft curve of her throat, his moving lips a sensuous flutter that finally ceased when he reached one warm taut breast. His tongue played gently with one nipple and Lee closed her eyes, feeling something inside her unfold like the petals of a flower teased open by the warmth of the sun.

It wasn't only his mouth, but his lean, hard body against her that aroused her softness into willing response. Her hands traveled the muscled expanse of his chest and stomach, her curved palms cupping his sides, riding along his hard ribs, his sensitive skin.

He rolled her over on her back and, propped up on one elbow, gazed down at her. Her eyes were held by the

186

startling classical purity of his male nakedness, the graceful symmetry of muscles and firm flesh. He moved on top of her, his flesh hot against her fingertips, making her shiver with its velvety hardness.

He leisurely explored her with his tongue and with his fingers in ways no man had ever done before.

"Oh, Paul, yes," she breathed as his hard flesh claimed her, the two becoming one.

"Love me, Paul," she whispered, made more alive by his hands, mouth, and thrusting body than she had ever been before. "Love me."

Paul loved her, his gentle hands molding her hips, moving with them as Lee responded willingly beneath them.

Finely tuned to each other's every move, together they climbed the heights of passion, and, when they could go no further, exploded together in a moment of ecstasy like nothing Lee had ever known. He held her tightly, as though afraid of losing her, and she clung to him, feeling a love greater than anything she would ever be able to put into words.

Later, when he was leaning against the headboard smoking a cigarette, his other arm cradling her, he asked her what she was thinking.

"I was thinking about what the *Post* critic said," Lee told him.

"What? You're thinking of critics at a time like this?"

"Well, I was thinking how much I loved you and I was also thinking about what he said."

He gave a low chuckle. "Indeed, a woman after my own heart. You mean about the courtroom procedure?"

She nodded.

"Yes, it could stand a little rewriting there."

"That's what I thought. But not tonight."

"Oh, no, not tonight. Most definitely not tonight," he said, stubbing out his cigarette, and once again gathering her up in his arms.

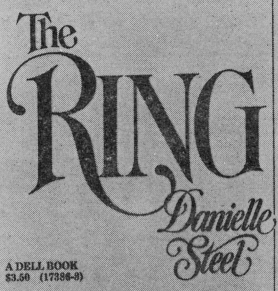

From the bestselling author of
Loving, **The Promise,** *and* **Palomino**

The RING

Danielle Steel

A DELL BOOK
$3.50 (17386-8)

A magnificent novel that spans this century's most dramatic years, *The Ring* **is the unforgettable story of families driven apart by passion—and brought together by enduring compassion and love.**

Love—the way you want it!

Candlelight Romances

Candlelight Ecstasy Romances

At your local bookstore or use this handy coupon for ordering:

Bestsellers

- [ ] **THE RING** by Danielle Steel $3.50 (17386-8)
- [ ] **INGRID BERGMAN: MY STORY**
  by Ingrid Bergman and Alan Burgess $3.95 (14085-4)
- [ ] **SOLO** by Jack Higgins $2.95 (18165-8)
- [ ] **THY NEIGHBOR'S WIFE** by Gay Talese....$3.95 (18689-7)
- [ ] **THE CRADLE WILL FALL** by Mary H. Clark $3.50 (11476-4)
- [ ] **RANDOM WINDS** by Belva Plain $3.50 (17158-X)
- [ ] **WHEN THE WIND BLOWS** by John Saul $3.50 (19857-7)
- [ ] **LITTLE GLORIA . . . HAPPY AT LAST**
  by Barbara Goldsmith $3.50 (15109-0)
- [ ] **CHANGE OF HEART** by Sally Mandel $2.95 (11355-5)
- [ ] **THE PROMISE** by Danielle Steel $3.50 (17079-6)
- [ ] **FLOWERS OF THE FIELD**
  by Sarah Harrison $3.95 (12584-7)
- [ ] **LOVING** by Danielle Steel $3.50 (14657-7)
- [ ] **CORNISH HEIRESS** by Roberta Gellis $3.50 (11515-9)
- [ ] **BLOOD RED WINE** by Laurence Delaney....$2.95 (10714-8)
- [ ] **COURT OF THE FLOWERING PEACH**
  by Janette Radcliffe $3.50 (11497-7)
- [ ] **FAIR WARNING**
  by George Simpson and Neal Burger $3.50 (12478-6)

At your local bookstore or use this handy coupon for ordering:

 DELL BOOKS
P.O. BOX 1000, PINEBROOK, N.J. 07058

Please send me the books I have checked above. I am enclosing $_____
(please add 75¢ per copy to cover postage and handling). Send check or money
order—no cash or C.O.D.'s. Please allow up to 8 weeks for shipment.

Mr/Mrs/Miss _____

Address _____

City _____ State/Zip _____